A₊

WITHDRAWN

PIÑON RANGE

**Center Point
Large Print**

**This Large Print Book carries the
Seal of Approval of N.A.V.H.**

PIÑON RANGE

LAURAN PAINE

Center Point Publishing
Thorndike, Maine

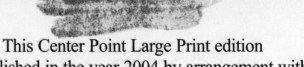

This Center Point Large Print edition
is published in the year 2004 by arrangement with
Golden West Literary Agency.

Copyright © 1976 by Lauran Paine in the British Commonwealth.
Copyright © 2004 by Mona Paine in the U.S.

All rights reserved.

The text of this Large Print edition is unabridged. In other
aspects, this book may vary from the original edition. Printed in
Thailand. Set in 16-point Times New Roman type.

ISBN 1-58547-459-2

Library of Congress Cataloging-in-Publication Data

Paine, Lauran.
    Piñon Range / Lauran Paine.--Center Point large print ed.
       p. cm.
    ISBN 1-58547-459-2 (lib. bdg. : alk. paper)
       1. Large type books. I. Title.

PS3566.A34P56 2004
813'.54--dc22

                                                            2004001604

1

THE FLAWLESS SKY

It was a rough, rolling land with piñon trees and sage. Its saving grace was its vastness, which made it awesome any time of the year and particularly spectacular in the spring, summer and autumn, but what prevented it from being simply a thousand-mile vastness of empty cow-country was the unique, tough, short-grass that arrived before the last freeze had departed and which lingered doggedly right on up into near-winter.

It never seemed to achieve a height of more than six or eight inches, and yet every grazing animal who browsed his way across it became greasy fat, with sleek, dark hair long before he quit the area, and livestock in particular did very well on that highly nutritious, uniquely localized dark green short-grass.

Matthew Wayland settled there in the early days, when every morning when a man went forth to feed he had to remove two bars from the inside of his cabin door, and had to wait five minutes until he had studied every tree and boulder before stepping out—and even then they sometimes scored a kill; if there was one thing a settler could say, back in those days, about the Apaches of northwestern Arizona Territory, it was that they never relented.

But old Matthew had been in his grave upon the hill east of the ranch many years by the time his grandson, George Wayland, met an equal challenge, and those

Apaches who had squatted out there with infinite patience just to get one fair shot at a white man, had been gone even longer. Some had returned, but they came back with a different outlook and the younger ones, most of whom had been born in the piñon country, worked the ranges as riders. It had taken an awful lot of blood and tragedy to create the meld, but it had been created.

George Wayland's rangeboss was a tall Apache named Ben Chavez. And that was another thing; back in old Matthew's day there had been extremely few tall Apaches.

Johnny Welton, the Wayland ranch's tophand, explained it this way: "When they quit existing on piñon nuts and lizards and commenced eating white-man beef, they commenced to quit bein' runts."

Ben's retort had been crisp and to the point. "That's right, Johnny, but until the white man was able to steal the piñon country for his cattle, they weren't worth eating."

There was another Indian who rode for the Wayland outfit. He was bandy-legged, wide-shouldered, thick-chested and had a face so flat he looked as though he had run head-on into a stone fence riding a running horse. His name was Jim Vargas and he resembled the old-time people, the *anasazi,* but as a matter of fact Jim Vargas was not an Apache, he was a Navajo. His people and Ben's people had long been enemies. The Navajos had been sedentary; they had farmed and worked hard. The Apaches had been raiders and plunderers.

Once, Jim mentioned this in the bunkhouse when

6

Johnny Welton and Wayland's other lanky pale-eyed rangerider, Cliff Howlett, had been discussing Indians. Jim had said, "It's always the same, isn't it? Folks who work for their living don't like folks who raid for their living." Jim had smiled, his jet-black eyes in their moonfaced setting showing narrowly and brightly. "I used to think us In'ians was a pretty sorry bunch of people until they taught me to read at the mission school and they gave me a history of Europe. Hell; us In'ians just played at it compared to you whiteskins."

Everyone had laughed, and when the Mexican cook rang his supper bell, they had trooped from the bunkhouse across the yard still amused.

The Wayland ranch was not the largest in the piñon country. That distinction belonged to an outfit owned by a family named Henrickson. Wayland ranch only employed four full-time riders on about twelve thousand acres of land where the Wayland tomahawk brand stood out upon something like three thousand head of cattle. Henrickson, by comparison, ran cattle the full westerly width of the piñon country, kept nine full-time rangeriders, and claimed over thirty thousand acres of land, but, like Wayland and everyone else, Henrickson did not run entirely upon deeded land. If the cattle drifted onto public domain so much the better; that way a cow outfit could save its own, deeded feed, until later in the year, and in the marginal piñon country which sometimes suffered prolonged droughts because of its proximity to the South Desert, it was standard policy to take every precaution in order not to be ruined should one of those droughts arrive.

The way George Wayland had learned from his father and grandfather, the best grass was saved for last, the cattle were drifted far off the deeded land as soon as there was enough provender to support them on the open range, and after three generations—this was the third one—it had become a proven system; if it hadn't, by now there would be no Henricksons and no George Wayland.

Then came the two-year drought.

Old-timers down around Cibola, the nearest town to the piñon cow country, could remember other two-year droughts, but none had arrived during George Wayland's tenure. He could recall any number of rainless long, parched summers, but invariably there had been winter rains to revive the land.

Not this year. The previous summer had been dry, and the rains had not come last winter. This spring when the grass came, it only got about three inches tall then began to wilt and wither.

Some cowmen over easterly hired the Zunis and Pueblos to work up their elaborate rain ritual. It hadn't rained a drop. They had even donated money to the priests at the mission down at Cibola to pray for relief, and presumably they had prayed because like all priests, they had not refused money, but it still had not rained.

There was a rumor of a rain-maker arriving over in some town a hundred miles away with his wagon full of special chemicals to color the smoke arising from his rain-making fires. Still not a drop of water fell.

The one thing which kept the cattle from dying by the

hundreds was that there was enough land so that even when their demands for grass required three and four times as much grazing country as before, they had that land to graze over.

The Henrickson outfit pushed their animals over through the bald hills more than a hundred miles northward, and left them to drift back slowly, grazing as they came.

George Wayland rode with his men and drifted his tomahawk cattle southwesterly to the limit of the short-grass country in that direction, and held them over against the rocky, rugged foothills of the Apache Peak country for two weeks before allowing them to start the drift back.

Drinking water was no problem, fortunately. The springs and dug-wells around the piñon country dropped, inevitably, but none of them actually went dry, and over along the foothills of the Apache Peak Territory there were a number of flowing springs.

Jim Vargas showed them one that even old Matthew had probably not known about. Jim knew about it, he told them, because as a small boy he had come over here to make meat with his family one summer. He even showed them several stone rings where the shelters had stood, and where the cooking-fires had been maintained.

Eventually, of course, they would also have water trouble if it did not rain the third year, but spring and summer came and merged with there still being plenty of water. In fact only the two-legged animals were desperate. The cattle and horses had to bite closer to the ground, but at least there was something to bite, so they did not noticeably suffer, although, again, unless relief arrived by autumn they would suffer. In fact, they would start wasting down to skin and bones, and eventually they would also begin to die.

It was this long-term condition that put men's tempers on edge, made their thoughts turn bitterly away from the beautiful but bone-dry sunrises each morning and the red-gold, bone-dry sunsets each evening.

Johnny Welton once summed it up over coffee at the foothill cowcamp against the Apache Peak slopes. "It's the gawddamned *helplessness*. We *know* what we need and we darned well know what's going to happen unless we get it—and there's not a lousy thing we can do about it but stand here and watch for clouds that don't never arrive."

That was true; but for the real effect of it, it had to be multiplied by each morning and each evening, every blessed spring and summer month. For two years.

George Wayland went down to Cibola with the wagon and returned three days later to the Apache Peak country with provisions. The only news he brought back with him was that there had been a stage robbery east of Cibola the previous week, and someone had told him the robbers were cowmen who had been broken and made destitute by the drought.

To that, the rangeboss Ben Chavez dryly said, "Sure. Everything that happens from now until it rains again is going to be blamed on bankrupted cowmen."

Probably, that was true enough.

It was pleasant over against the mountains. If they

hadn't been living day by day with their worry and their desperation it would have been a very enjoyable time for them all.

There was game to be shot, a variety of it, and George had brought back two bottles of old popskull from town with him, so they laced their coffee in the evenings around the fire, and although the grass disappeared a little more each day that passed and the cattle tried to drift away from the foothills requiring a little more hard riding each day, it was a cool camp with good water nearby and while the days got increasingly hot as summer advanced, each night was an awesome panoply of hushed, brilliant and endless magnificence.

The problem was that they could not really enjoy the camp. Jim Vargas told Ben Chavez one afternoon when they rode in to take turns upending the *olla* to cut the scorch from parched gullets that maybe their salvation lay in pushing the cattle on up into the mountains and letting them forage for themselves; there was grass in the canyons, and springwater and shade.

Ben handed back the *olla* with his principal objection. "Yeah. There are also bears and wolves and cougars. It'd be a choice between *maybe* losing the herd to starvation and drought out here, or *sure as hell* losing it back in there to predators."

Jim did not argue about it. He rarely argued at all, about anything. He was a thoughtful, capable, willing man, as homely as a mud fence but thoroughly honest and dependable and generous.

If his idea was no good at least it proved that he was trying just as hard as George Wayland was trying, to also come up with a solution to their increasingly ominous dilemma.

They all were trying to come up with a solution. So were the Henrickson riders, so were all the cowmen and riders across the entire drought-area, but there was really only one practical solution—rainfall—and every morning when hundreds of eyes looked upwards first thing, there was that beautiful, pale azure sky without a cloud in it, without a single flaw as far as anyone could see.

2

STRANGERS!

When George decided to allow the cattle to begin their drift he estimated that it would require six weeks for them to get back to their home range. With that much respite, he would have the time he needed to devise his next retrenching step.

If there was another retrenching step.

They pitched bedrolls and camp-gear into the wagon on the ninth day, which was the absolute maximum they could hold the cattle against the slopes, and by the time the sun arose they had the team on the pole, their saddle animals rigged out, and were ready to ride.

The cattle were miles northward and miles southward foraging up the wide, shallow little canyons. By the time they discovered their herders had departed it would be mid-day and they seldom moved when the sun was directly above. That was their time for seeking shade, lying patiently in it chewing their cuds, and waiting until late afternoon to lumber up onto all fours and go foraging again.

This time, with no horsemen to hold them, they would start the drift towards home-range country.

The men were at a spring called Blue Sump because of some blue stone beneath the water which gave it a pleasant appearance, watering their horses, when Ben Chavez wrinkled his nose and looked slowly in all directions. He said he smelled cattle.

Cliff Howlett sniffed and shook his head. He did not smell a blasted thing he said, except maybe a little brimstone. They chuckled, forgot about the supposed odor and struck out again on tanked-up mounts.

The sun was high and hot but they were accustomed to heat. Only two of them, Chavez and Vargas, were pigmented for it but the others, the whiteskins, were bronzed enough to be pretty well immune. They had canteens but it would take more heat and a longer ride than this to make them use that kind of water.

Cliff Howlett and Johnny Welton got to arguing over the possibility of a rain-maker bringing relief. Howlett said he'd seen rain-makers cause downpours in Indian Territory, and Johnny Welton said, hell, if it rained, then it was going to rain anyway.

Vargas and Chavez rode with George, on either side of the wagon, looking amused but maintaining absolute silence.

It was George who finally put an end to that discussion. He leaned to look back, and called Ben Chavez up to him beside the wagon.

"I didn't smell anything back yonder, but I sure do now. Ride out and around, Ben. Take Jim with you. I sure as hell smell cattle."

It was something they all thought about. It occurred to them, of course, that while they had been gone over against the westerly slopes doing their utmost to save the home-place feed, it would be a genuine disaster if someone else had drifted cattle over their home-place feed.

No one mentioned this as Ben and Jim rode away, one rider angling northeasterly the other one angling southeasterly, but they thought of it because it was the only thing imaginable which would have produced that strong smell.

The land looked empty, but of course they were still miles from home; in fact Blue Sump marked the approximate westerly boundary of Wayland range.

That was another thing they rode along thinking about. If they could smell cattle this far west, if someone had actually drifted a herd across the home-place, then it had to be a large herd for the scent to travel that far, and that was something else to worry about.

There was a bosque of trees beside an erosion arroyo a mile and a half east of Blue Sump where they drew rein to let the horses blow a little, although the horses were not the least bit tired. When the wagon halted, the riders with it also halted. All three of them rolled cigarettes, but as a matter of fact, with Cliff Howlett it was simply a matter of being courteous when he was offered the makings. Normally, he did not smoke, he chewed.

Eventually they saw Jim Vargas miles deep sitting his horse, a thick, coarse lump atop a wide, sturdy saddle animal. "Sees something," stated Johnny Welton. "They got a habit; one of 'em will see something and sit like a bump on a log not moving or making a sound for minutes on end, studying it. Ben does that, too."

George reached for the canteen at the back of the boot beneath his feet. He drank, and offered the canteen around but got no acceptances. Cliff and Johnny were watching Vargas very intently, cigarette smoke drifting up, out and around the greasy, curled brims of their hats.

"Comin' back," said Johnny. "Sure as hell he saw something he didn't like. He's riding kind of hard for a hot day like this."

George picked up additional movement, but southward and out even further. For a while he could only make out that something was approaching, but by the time Jim was almost within recognizable distance, he made it out as a horse and rider. He pointed it out to Johnny and Cliff.

"Ben, most likely," suggested Cliff, but they could not be certain until Jim Vargas was well within their sight, so evidently the rangeboss had covered a lot more ground than Jim had.

Vargas slackened gait a mile out and walked his horse on in. As he swung off in the shade to loosen the cinch and allow his horse a moment or two to rest and catch his breath, the squatty, moon-faced, greasy-dark Navajo said, "It's cattle, George, and it's a hell of a herd of them. They been rangin' over our grass, from the looks of the sign on the ground, maybe a week or so.

Johnny smashed out his cigarette atop the saddlehorn with a fiery curse. "Whose mark?" he snapped, but Vargas had no answer to that.

"I didn't get up that close. There was a couple of riders dead ahead of me, and they was both armed with saddleguns and pistols." Jim looked steadily at his employer from narrowed, jet-black eyes. "Free-grazers, George?"

Wayland had no way of knowing but it was a reasonable assumption that it was free-graze-men, those scourges of every organized, developed open-range territory, because they simply drove overland and never stopped, their herds eating up all the grass as they went.

Ben Chavez did not slacken pace until he was only a short distance out, and even then he acted reluctant about favoring the horse. When he got up where the others could see his face it was shiny with sweat, the lips pulled flat back, and the black eyes blazing with anger. Ben had the Apache temperament but he was also a strong-willed man; when he got this angry it was usually with justification. He looked past at Jim Vargas and snarled something in a guttural way. The Navajo shrugged thick shoulders and turned to look at his horse. Whatever the rangeboss had said, Jim had evidently understood it but had not liked it. Another Navajo would have understood Jim's turning away: Navajos considered the losing of one's temper the worst indication of an unruly disposition; it embarrassed them.

George said, "What is it?" to his rangeboss, and while

Ben stepped off and reached to savagely loosen his cincha, he said, "Cattle. Hundreds of them on our grass. They've eaten it down, George." Ben turned, a white line showing above his upper lip. "There is a wagon down there a couple, three miles, with a remuda of saddle-stock out back. It looks like they came onto our range about the same time we took our cattle to the mountains." Ben paused, looked balefully at the others, then sucked down a big breath and noisily expelled it. Along with it went his first furious flash of temper. He faced Jim. "What did you see, *compadre?*"

Vargas turned and answered shortly, re-telling for the second time what had held his attention. Then he added something else. "When we chase them off—what about the grass? It's gone."

That was what George Wayland was sitting on the wagon-seat thinking about. Ten days over against the mountains to conserve this, and someone had come along and grazed it off. He was this close to being ruined. It did not require much more than something like this, under the circumstances, to ruin a cowman.

Cliff Howlett said, "Ride for Cibola, George, swear out an impound against them fellers and hold their damned cattle until they pay for the grass."

Johnny looked pained. "Free-grazers never have a second cent to bless themselves with, and you'd ought to know that, Cliff."

"Then claim their gawddamned cattle," stated Howlett, reddening slightly at Johnny's disparaging tone of voice.

Johnny agreed with that. "Only thing to do," he said,

and looked at George Wayland. "Claim 'em by law, sell 'em at auction, and maybe you can still come out, George."

Wayland looked around caustically. "Who is going to buy?" he asked. "Henrickson? Shaffer? Campbell over east of Cibola? Who wants any more cattle on their range, when they can't even feed their own?"

George lifted his lines and clucked up the team. As they started away from the shade-trees, a rider far out loped onto the horizon facing them, halted and sat like a carving for several minutes, then whirled and loped back out of sight.

No one said a word among the men returning from the Apache Peak country, but they all thought pretty much the same thing as they slouched along through the still, dazzling sunlight.

They saw the cattle, finally when they had traversed another two miles, but none of them were close enough for their brands to be readable. Ben would have loped out for a closer inspection but George told him to stay with the wagon.

There were armed riders with those strange cattle. As Jim Vargas had noted, they wore the customary belt gun, but they also carried saddleguns, and that was unusual among rangeriders out simply keeping track of cattle, unless of course they expected trouble or were in varmint-country.

Something those strangers did which impressed the men riding back from Apache Peak—they stayed away; they patently saw the Wayland-ranch crew and sat their horses watching every step the Wayland-riders took, but never once offered to come within rifle-range.

"That's no damned accident," stated Cliff Howlett, surlily. "They either know who we are or they guessed, and they ain't going to come over here—for a darned good reason. They didn't accidentally come onto our grass when we was gone and eat it down to the dust; they know right well how we are feeling about now and they're not going to ride over here within gunshot range."

Ben Chavez counted the riders. "Nine," he said. "That couldn't be Henrickson, could it? He's got nine riders."

Johnny Welton snorted. "Henrickson's a *cow*man man, Ben. He wouldn't do a thing like this."

They had the buildings in sight and had crossed through the strange herd by the time the sun was lowering. The last couple of miles they scarcely spoke at all. When they reached the yard George jumped down, passed the lines to Ben Chavez and without a word headed for the cookshack.

But the Mexican cook was not there. In fact he was nowhere on the ranch and they all looked for him high and low, eventually, after they had parked the wagon, cared for their animals, and chucked their camp gear upon stripped bunks southward from the Wayland-house at the log-and-adobe bunkhouse.

"Scairt off," said Johnny Welton. "For every Messican who don't scare easy there's a hundred and fifty that do." Johnny looked at George, then said, "I'll make supper." He turned to cross the yard, then slowly halted and turned back. "And anybody who don't like it, can go to hell."

Johnny was a good cook. Surprisingly so, in fact, and even George, with all his other causes for worry, mentioned something about this, along with all the other Wayland-riders, but Johnny Welton did not say where he had learned to cook, all he said was, "It's got to be a genuine emergency. The cook's got to be dead or dying or we all got to be starving. I don't hire out except for riding."

George arose and went out upon the porch to smoke and when the others drifted out to join him he said, "I'm going to clean up, then ride down to Cibola. We've got to do this right; we're not going to just bust over there and shoot up their wagon and their camp. That would land us in more trouble than it would land them in. Those days passed along with my grandfather."

Cliff Howlett gravely said, "There was a heap to be said in favor of how them old-timers handled things like this," and whittled off a corner of cut-plug to pouch up into one cheek before closing and pocketing his wicked-blade big stockman's clasp-knife. "But you're the boss, George." He sighed. "I'll help you catch a fresh animal and rig it out."

As those two walked down off the cookshack porch and across the evening-lighted yard Jim Vargas looked at the rangeboss. "I could ride out a little and back," he said quietly.

Chavez nodded. "Go. Wait until George has gone, then go."

3

WAYLAND'S WAY

There was no moon but there was enough starshine to compensate for the lost light when Johnny called on all those who had eaten his meal to march the hell back inside the cookshack and help do up the pots, pans, and dishes.

They all went except Jim, who had disappeared in the darkness out the rear of the barn, and the men in the lighted cookshack did not even mention Jim's name. They did not act as though someone named Jim Vargas even existed.

Later, when they doused the light at the cookshack and trooped across the yard to the bunkhouse to begin sorting out camping gear and create order in their bunkhouse again, someone suggested a game of stud, and eventually they sat around the long bunkhouse table with its carved initials, rowel-marks and ingrained stains, still declining to discuss the absence of Jim Vargas although as they tiredly sat playing poker, they were doing this for only one real reason; to kill time until Vargas returned.

He came back as soundlessly as he had vanished, thick and squatty, flat-faced and menacing in appearance, but actually a kindly, affable, shrewd individual. They got him a cup of java and made a place for him at the table.

"Nine," he told them, looking at Ben Chavez. "Like

you figured. They got no less than twenty-five horses over there in that rope corral, and they've got a pretty big old wagon." He cursed because the coffee had burned him and shoved the cup away. "They talk like Texans. In the light of their cooking fire they show plenty of guns. I tried to get in close enough to really hear them talking but I couldn't; there wasn't any decent cover. Just a word now and then. I think they were talking about us, though. Their *jefe is* an old man—grey and bushy-headed and as big as a horse. He wears a coat at the campfire with his gunbelt around the outside side of it. Like he was expecting trouble. Maybe he was; they saw us today, they got to know this here is our range they've grazed off."

Ben Chavez scratched his coal-black head and ruefully eyed the Navajo. "A rope corral?"

Jim's bright black eyes went to Chavez's face and did not move off it for a long while. He very slowly smiled. "It broke," he said. "I whittled on it. A clean cut and they'd know."

Cliff scoffed. "They'll know anyway, Jim. They seen us pass along today, they'll know who we are—now their rope corral busts."

Johnny said, "What's the difference? Let the bastards know. Let 'em show up over here to complain."

No one argued with that truculent logic, but Chavez said, "George wants it done by the law."

"My butt," growled Cliff scornfully. "The law's not going to do a damned thing in time to save what grass is left. The law never moved fast in its lousy life."

There was a momentary silence, then Jim Vargas

22

dropped a bombshell. "They got a woman over there, in their camp. A young woman, and she's not their cook."

They looked steadily at him for a while trying to adjust to this announcement. "The old man's wife?" asked Johnny, and Jim looked doubtful.

"Too young."

"Then she's his daughter," said Cliff, but began to doubt his own statement as soon as he had made it. "Why would a free-graze-man bring his daughter along when he's trespassing and heading into trouble?"

No one answered until Jim Vargas said, "Maybe she's the big old man's daughter, but I'll tell you one thing about her: She wears a gun just like the men do. She dresses like a rider. I think she's one of them; I think when they go out she rides right along with them."

They sat around drinking coffee, smoking and enjoying heat from the bunkhouse stove because the night turned off a little cooler than most summertime nights had been up until now, and they pondered the information that Jim had brought back from his nocturnal scouting trip.

None of it really astonished them, except the part about the girl free-graze rider. That was unusual enough for them to sit and discuss it for a full hour before someone arose with a groan and curse and headed for his bunk.

By the time George Wayland got back, not too long before sunrise, they had all been bedded down for a long while. George cared for his animal, trooped over to the cookshack just in case there was still some coffee in the pot, and after losing out on that, went along to his mainhouse and also turned in.

But for George the rest was very brief. Cibola was a middling-long ride from the ranch, just going in. Going in then coming back was twice as long and twice as tiring.

Especially when all he had accomplished he explained in two sentences at breakfast the next morning. "I found Pedro," he reported to the riding crew, "at a Mex cantina over in back of town and he was afraid so he refused to come back and cook. He said he saw those strangers scout up the ranch last week and that was when he abandoned the ranch and came down to Cibola.

"As for the law, Jud Porter said his authority ends at the town limits. He agreed to send out a telegram for the U.S. marshal over at Albuquerque, but he said the last time he had to do that, the deputy marshal didn't reach Cibola for a month. So . . ."

Cliff Howlett reached for the coffee as he said, "I told you yesterday those old-timers had the best way of handling this kind of thing. I still think they had." He poured his cup full and pushed the pot away. "We can ride over there this morning."

George said, "*I'll* ride over there this morning."

Cliff was unrelenting. "They aren't going to pull out because one man, not even the owner himself, tells them to. George; we could sort of drift along and set out a ways, guns handy."

Ben Chavez looked at his employer with a faint expression of exasperation. "You'd have backing if you needed it."

24

George smiled at Ben. "First, we'll do it my way. If that don't work, Ben . . ." He kept on smiling but did not finish the sentence. They were all placated, somewhat anyway although Cliff still looked dourly forbidding as he drank his coffee then arose to clear away his dishes and help wash up and clean the kitchen.

When they got down to the barn Johnny was pulling on his gloves when he said, "Hey; I don't think my hands ever been this clean before. Maybe washin' dishes is good for a feller's skin."

"Soak your head in it," mumbled Cliff, "maybe it'll make you smart."

George told them to hunt up the saddle-stock and bring them in, and not to separate in their hunt for them. He did not explain why he did not want them to ride separately but there could have been several reasons, all of them having to do with George's desire to avoid trouble, if it could be avoided.

When he swung across leather and rode out of the yard they dolefully watched his departure, and Jim Vargas had a comment to offer.

"That's what don't make sense; when you know there's going to be trouble, just one white man riding out."

The others may have agreed but they said nothing. They trooped around back to snake out saddle-stock for their horse-hunt.

George viewed this matter of approaching the trespassers differently. He knew, because he had seen it happen a number of times, that when there was valid reason for antagonism, when a band of armed rangemen rode out to brace an equally as yeasty a band of the same kind of men, trouble resulted and it was not uncommon for burials to ensue.

He intended to get those strangers off his range, and he intended to see that they made some kind of suitable arrangement for the amount of his grass their cattle had used up, but he only meant to accomplish those things with guns as an absolute last resort.

His grandfather would have listened, would have pondered, then would have gruffly said, "He's young," and would have rounded up the riding crew and gone out there to burn the wagon, scatter the free-graze cattle far and wide, and bury as many of those free-graze people as he possibly could. He would not accept a penny of their money, either. In his grandfather's day a man did not allow himself to be bought off.

George rolled a smoke, loped overland in the clear, fragrant morning enjoying the smoke, the scenery, the beauty of the new, glass-clear day, and tried not to think about the imminence of disaster which was waiting just beyond tomorrow to ruin him.

When he finally had the wagon in sight there was a team harnessed already and made fast to the tongue, the tailgate was up and chained for traveling, and four of those nine free-grazers were sitting their saddles ready to move out.

They saw him at about the same time he saw them. Word was passed. He could see that happening as the riders out there turned one at a time to look back towards where he was coming out of the sunshine.

He saw no woman, and as a matter of fact had no

reason to believe there was one; sometimes men wore their hair long and from a distance Jim Vargas could have been mistaken.

But he wasn't.

A rawboned, shaggy-headed man riding a big roan gelding turned to ride out and head George off. The other riders also turned but the man on the roan growled at them and waved them back towards the wagon.

George saw the jutting Winchester-butt on the far side of the rawboned-man's saddle-swells and when they were close enough to each other he also noticed that this big, rawboned older man did not have a tie-down thong on his sixgun. There was no tie-down threaded through his holster at all.

George drew rein to walk his horse the last few yards, while the older man halted and sat stonily, hands lightly lying atop his saddlehorn making his judgment.

The older man was hard and dangerous, none too clean, unshorn and bristly-faced. He looked mean and troublesome. George swung his horse a little and halted, completed his study of the older man, then said, "My name is George Wayland. I own the land you've been running your herd on. I want the cattle off by tomorrow, and I want some kind of a decent settlement for my grass.

The older man's craggy face showed nothing, nor did he speak right away. He continued to sit there studying George, and finally he ranged a searching look elsewhere, out and around, as though he were suspicious that George had not really arrived alone, as though he half-expected an ambush. Then he finally said, "Mister;

if it ain't fenced it's free-graze," and that statement settled the question for George as to what these people
were. Free-grazers, some of the most thoroughly dis-
liked stockmen who ever forked a horse or choused a
cow.

George's retort was cold. "Not in this country, that
don't apply, mister. What will it be: You pay for the
grass and clear out before tomorrow night, or neither?"

The older man leaned aside and spat amber, straight-
ened up and continued to study George as though he
were having trouble arriving at a conclusion about
something. Finally, as he raised his reinhand as though
to turn away, he said, "Neither; and sonny don't you
touch that pistol, 'cause the way us folks live, right now
there's at least three rifles—not no damned little saddleguns, real *rifles*—pointin' out this far waitin' for you
to make a mistake." The older man spat again, shifted
his cud and said, "Don't you try and impound no lightning cattle, neither, sonny. We know who you are and
how many fellers ride for you, and we sure-Lord got
you outnumbered, out-figured, and if you want, we'll
out-fight you."

George had nothing more to say. He and the older
man regarded one another for a while, then George
looked farther back, over around the wagon—and
hell—there was a girl over there leaning across a big
rear wagonwheel with a long-barreled rifle in her
hands, snugged back and aimed directly at him.

He was surprised. The older free-grazer cast one last
look his way, then rode back, but before he did this he
said, "You fellers come skulkin' around here again in

the night cuttin' our corral ropes, sonny, and there's going to be some gawddamned settler-hides fleshed-out and nailed to the trees.

"Sonny, we was breakin' cowmen like you to lead before you was born. Me and my kinsmen. As for bein' off your land; we're goin'. We was fixin' to pull out last night. We never stay once the grass is eat off."

George studied those riders over around the wagon. He was for a fact, under several of those long-barreled rifles, and what intrigued him was the way those people had done that; without a word passing among them, as though they did things like this just naturally.

Which they did; free-grazers were the enemies of everyone. Not just established cowmen like George Wayland, but even townfolk; merchants whom they never paid and people on the outskirts of the towns they passed whose milk-cows had a way of disappearing when a band of free-grazers passed through.

4

A HIGH, BLACK SKY

Ben Chavez's temper showed but he listened to what George had to say and did not interrupt, did not in fact utter a sound until George had told them what the big old shaggy-headed free-grazer had said, then Ben made a little squirting laugh and glanced at the other riders before saying, "The son of a bitch is going to ride off just like that—and you're out of grass, George, and the rest of us is out of jobs." He settled his black eyes upon

29

his employer. "I figure I'd better quit or you'd better fire me, because I don't think you handled them right, and now I got an itch to do it another way."

Cliff Howlett agreed with that. "A man grazes off your grass down to the nubbins, then dares you to do something about it; I agree with Ben. He's got a settlin'-up coming."

George surprised them by agreeing. "Seems like he has, for a fact." And while his outraged and indignant riders digested that, in surprise, he also said, "Now that you've got the horses in off the range and our cattle are ten miles to the west, the only livestock on our range are those lightning-branded cattle of the free-grazers. It's a little late today to start it, but first thing in the morning we're going to sashay out and round up a band or two of those critters, drive them over here to the range around the buildings, and impound them."

Johnny Welton had a question. "You got an impound-order in Cibola last night?"

George smiled. "Nope. Didn't more than mention impounding when I was talking to Jud Porter. We'll just make a judge Colt impound."

Ben looked placated. "They'll come shooting," he surmised. "Did you see a girl over there?"

George looked squarely at his rangeboss and did not answer the question. "Who went out there last night," he asked, "and cut their rope corral?"

The four rangemen became very busy either looking for hangnails on their work-roughened hands, or peering into the great vault of heaven seeking a hint of a raincloud. No one answered and George did not press the issue.

They went out behind the barn to look over the remuda of saddle-stock. There were a lot of bare-footed horses back there, and Johnny Welton groaned because he knew what George was going to say, and Johnny did not like shoeing horses.

That is how they spent the balance of the day, shoeing, cuffing, readying the loose-stock for use, and when Johnny finally legitimately got clear of the hard, hazardous, difficult work by heading for the cookshack to start supper, not even sarcastic Cliff Howlett said anything. There were not very many unwritten rules around a ranch-yard, but irritating the cook was one of them. No one enjoyed burnt meals and ranch-cooks were a notoriously vindictive, mean lot.

They used up the balance of the day preparing for what they intended to do the following day, and shortly before dusk George sent Ben out to scout the range for a couple of miles. He knew about how long it would take those free-graze people to round up all those lightning-branded cattle of theirs, and he knew about how far they'd get before dusk or nightfall halted them, but he wanted to be sure. His private estimate was that they would get about half way along from where he had seen them in camp this morning, to Blue Sump. They would still be on his range by several miles come morning. He *wanted* them to still be on his land.

Ben returned after dark to report that the free-grazers had not even made that much good time. Ben thought the reason for the delay was because they hadn't been able to catch all their loose saddle-stock until fairly late this morning. They certainly would not leave Wayland-range without their saddle-stock.

At supper that evening the men spoke freely and casually. With the possible exception of Johnny Welton they had all been involved in affairs like this on the range; things men never talked about afterwards. They had rules and laws which were not very different from the rules and laws defined and outlined in the law books, but they had different ideas about enforcing them.

Right now, over Johnny's supper, they smoked and talked, and did not once mention that everything from this point on had to be absolutely secret. They *knew* without discussing it what the penalties were; that what they were about to do was illegal. That did not stop them any more than it stopped anyone else who did something which was against the law. Bullets and hang-ropes, and sometimes but not very often prison, stopped lawbreakers, but talk never stopped them.

Ben and Jim volunteered to scout up the nearest free-graze cattle. George was willing; like everyone else in the cookshack he was ready to believe a pair of buck-Indians could track better, could do a job of scouting-up better than the rest of them could.

They washed their dishes and went across to the bunkhouse when darkness was down, and George lingered a while in the loneliness of his main-house veranda smoking and trying to predict how this was going to end. He did not think about his grandfather; if he had he would have made a wry face: The old man would have gone to bed tonight and slept like a baby, then would have arisen ahead of firstlight in the morning, buckled on his gunbelt, picked up his hat, his jacket and his booted Winchester, and would have ridden out there to kill men.

The old man would not have impounded any cattle. He probably did not even know what that word meant. But he would have had a re-branding bee in the cold, blustery autumn weather, and as many of those rebranded lightning-branded cattle as could have survived a Montana winter would have come to grass the following springtime wearing Wayland's tomahawk.

George grinned a trifle ruefully, stamped out his cigarette and went inside to bed down. The old man had done a whale of a lot of things a man could no longer do. Maybe that was why a man was not permitted to outlive his time; if *he* had lived on into this present generation, the old devil would have the ranch and its riders in hot water all the time.

George's last thought before he dozed off was: I'm not doing a damned bit different! And it was true.

Someone rattling the side window awakened George in the darkness. He knew, before his eyes were fully open, who it was. When he grumbled the familiar tone of his rangeboss came softly through the windowglass.

"Jim and I're ready to ride out. Johnny's fixin' breakfast. We'll be back directly."

George lay back staring into the darkness. He blew out a big, ragged breath, heaved himself upright and swung his feet to the cold floor. That contact finished the awakening process for him.

The night was still fully dominant, there were stars like flung-back diamonds across the total blackness as far and farther than a man could see, when George got dressed standing by the window.

There was a light at the cookshack and one at the bunkhouse. He irrelevantly thought that unless he hired a cook soon now, Johnny would probably quit altogether.

He reached for his hefty bulletbelt and holstered Colt as he agreed with himself that on his next trip to town he would find a cook and fetch him back to the ranch.

He did not go directly to the cookshack. He never did that; his first round every morning included a crossing of the yard and an inspection of the corralled and stalled livestock.

This morning everything had been fed.

He crossed to the cookshack and found Cliff Howlett helping Johnny get the morning meal. Cliff was a rough, direct, craggy individual but he was also co-operative, and that was primarily what had inclined George Wayland to keep him on.

Johnny nodded his "good-morning" and pointed to the coffeepot. "Fresh batch," he said, then went back to the frying breakfast steaks and potatoes.

Cliff finished laying out the food. He was working with a cud of chewing tobacco in his cheek, which was something George and a lot of other cowmen stood in awe of—a man who could take on a big load of chewing tobacco first thing in the morning.

Cliff already had his gun and belt buckled on. Johnny was slick-hipped. George did not feel so out-of-place after all. When Cliff slid a platter in front of George he said, "They'll make it neat as a pin. On a black morning you can't see their damned black hides anyway. And they're good at skulking. Ben'll be better than Jim, just naturally."

Johnny came to the table with another pair of platters, shoved one at Cliff and sat down with the other plate. There was enough food for breakfast to last most men the full day, and this had been a thought in the back of Johnny's mind when he was planning the meal. Mostly, a man could surmise about how long he would have to exist between meals, but then, usually, work on a cow ranch was more or less predictable. Not today.

Johnny started to eat without paying the least attention to his companions, but when Cliff continued to talk Johnny finally turned and said, "Why don't you just shut up and eat; what good is a cold chunk of steak?"

Cliff subsided. The three of them said almost nothing until they distinctly heard shod horses crossing hardpan out in the yard.

"Now we'll know," muttered Cliff, and reared back to refill his coffeecup.

They had a long wait but that too was predictable. Chavez and Vargas had their horses to look after before entering the cookshack.

Johnny went after two more platters of food and was returning to the table with them when the tall, tawny rangeboss entered and directly behind him the darker, squattier and much heavier Navajo walked in, blinking against the steady glow of lamplight.

Johnny pointed. "Eat. It's still hot. Eat first before it

gets cold, then talk."

Vargas was willing to obey that injunction but the rangeboss wasn't. He stepped over the bench, though, sat down and picked up his knife and fork, then wrinkled his nose in appreciation, but before he went to work on the steak he said, "We got a bunch picked out. We'll lead you out there in a little while. There wasn't no one around; we scouted high and low." Ben leaned to start cutting the meat. "I was sure, after they had their run in with you today, George, they'd have nighthawks out." He looked across at Jim as though expecting support. He got it.

"Not a man with that little band. I looked around for an hour." Vargas was more philosophical about such a thing. "Maybe they don't figure on us doing nothing. Maybe they don't know they got that little bunch cut off from their main herd." He shrugged beefy shoulders and returned to his meal.

Cliff was scowling. "What do you mean by a little bunch? Ten, thirty head; fifty maybe?"

"Couple hundred," said the rangeboss, "more or less."

That seemed to satisfy them all, even Cliff. No one said anything for a while, not until George arose with a lighted cigarette in his hand and strolled to a window to look out into the yard, and farther, out across the night-stained westerly piñon country.

"I'll be down at the barn," he told them, and walked out of the cookshack. Cliff and Johnny gulped down the dregs of their java and also headed out. Ben and Jim continued eating as though there was no hurry; they had earned the right and they intended to make the most of it, but eventually they too picked up their hats and stalked out into the cold darkness. Ben sniffed; it was getting as cold as it would be for the next twenty-four hours; what that meant was that dawn was not too far off, perhaps a couple of hours.

Ben said, "We can make it," and Jim Vargas grunted approval as they strode over where someone had lighted the barn lamp so they could all see while they saddled up, bridled their mounts, and buckled the saddleboots into place.

Johnny was humming but none of the other men made a sound. Maybe Johnny felt like humming but no one else did.

George led his horse forth, turned it, and swung up across cold leather on the last turn. The horse humped his back a little, like a lot of ranch-horses do when they have a cold blanket and saddle on their backs first thing in the morning, but that's all he did, which was just as well because George had his romal raised and his spurs poised.

Ben pointed the way and led off out of the yard. All around them there was brittle cold darkness, except for the lamp still burning at the cookshack and over at the bunkhouse.

5

ROUNDUP!

They rode heads-up. Not a one of them had any illusions about the reaction of the free-graze riders if they encountered the Wayland riding crew driving off their beef. It would not matter one iota that the Wayland riders were within their rights as long as they were on their own land.

They talked very little. Mostly, they walked their horses, except for a mile or two of slow-loping, and they listened, but there was nothing to be heard for a long while, not until Ben Chavez grunted them down to a halt and pointed into the onward darkness.

By then every man among them could smell the cattle.

It was, as they had discussed back at the cookshack, a band of roughly two hundred head. Why they had not been gathered during the course of the general free-graze roundup, was anyone's guess, but the fact remained they hadn't, and as George quietly ordered his men to start riding out and around to complete the partial surround, he instructed them to look closely for horsemen; it was his feeling that if the free-grazers had spent most of yesterday looking for their cattle and heading them on westerly, they may not have had enough daylight to complete the gather and bring in this band. But he also felt that if this were so, sure as hell there would be free-grazers coming after these cattle today.

His idea was to have them back over by his home-place by the time the free-grazers came looking for them.

His men were old hands. They skirted far out and around the bedded animals, chousing only a few old fighting mossbacks up out of their beds with snorts and lowered heads.

The actual drive was not begun until the men had very cautiously scouted the area, then had come down in behind the bedded beasts. George heard them stamping up out of their beds and knew the drive was on its way. He remained to one side, southward, saw Johnny Welton taking the point, saw Johnny's white face turned in his direction, and flagged an encouraging signal which Johnny acknowledged.

The cattle made very little noise. If they had been wet cows it would have been different; they would have set up a caterwauling for their calves which could have been heard for miles.

There was another distinct advantage: Free-graze cattle were constantly being herded, being driven here and there by men on horseback. A lot of range cattle only saw mounted men twice a year and got to be as wild as coyotes, but not these cattle; they had been plodding ahead of drovers ever since they had been owned by the free-grazers. The sight of mounted men pushing in close was anything but a novelty to them; they trooped along without lowing, without trying to cut back, because they were completely accustomed to moving in this fashion.

George rode on the south edge of the herd and occasionally drifted in fairly close to examine his charges. They were not especially breedy animals; every one that George could see had a wicked span of horns, slab-sides, a big, long dolorous face, and a backbone like the ridgepole of a tent. Texas cattle, rangemen called them. Longhorns. They would fight a bear, a man afoot or ahorseback, a mountain lion or a buzz-saw, if they were roiled up. Many a good rangeman had died beneath their stone-hard sharp hooves in a race not very many horses ever won—out in front of a stampede.

On the other hand they could weather-out a Montana blizzard, and come through strong because they would emulate elk and deer and wapiti; they would eat tree-leaves and tree-bark when the grass was covered under three feet of snow, which was a characteristic the breedier, better-quality range cattle did not do, hence they died of starvation by the hundreds every winter.

Still, most stockmen had been trying to breed-out the Texas strain for many years, and that was another thing George did not like to think about; all those mangy, slab-sided, mean-eyed Texas bulls pairing off with his upgraded cattle.

Johnny Welton drifted over to within shouting distance and cupped his hands. "George! We got boot-leather and nothin' else!"

George smiled and nodded his head without answering. Off in the distant east the sky was beginning to pull back slightly to disclose a thin line of watery grey light the full length of the uneven horizon. They had perhaps another hour of darkness.

It should be enough. Texas cattle were leggier than

grade-critters; if they had to or if they were made to, Texas cattle could walk a hole in the day—or the night.

George rolled and lit a smoke, snugged up his jacket to prevent the cold from seeping inside from around his gullet, twisted to ride a short distance looking rearward, and when he seemed satisfied and faced forward again, that sliver of fish-belly grey along the rim of the world had widened another couple of inches.

Ben Chavez loped ahead looking for George. When they met Ben said, "Jim's shagging back a mile or so. We thought we heard something back there."

George was skeptical. "How—with all these cattle rattling horns and walking along?"

Ben conceded with a shrug. "Jim went back anyway," he said, then rode along eyeing the breaking of dawn. "We'll make it," he opined and turned to go back where he had been, and pick up Vargas to help keep the herd hiking right along.

They had the buildings dimly in sight against the brightening eastern heavens when Johnny Welton eased over to George to say, "They're going to be madder'n wet hens." He smiled about that, mischievously.

Where they slacked off and allowed the Texas cattle to fan out a little, there was fair grass because they never grazed off the territory this close to the buildings until they knew full winter was nigh. That way, even if they had deep snowdrifts, they could keep an eye on the cattle as they pawed down to grass.

The Texas cattle would probably not drift for several days, not when they had better feed now than they had had before. By George's calculation several days was about all he would need to bring this matter to a conclusion, one way or the other.

The free-graze men had one option George's tomahawk-crew lacked a genuine defense against. They could ride up very quietly in the night, get behind their impounded cattle, and suddenly start shouting and shooting. Texas cattle would stampede at the drop of a hat. The trick of course was to be sure and stampede the Texas cattle westerly, in the right direction, because if the cattle went in the opposite direction they would be deeper than ever on Wayland-range.

Desperate men did desperate things; stampeding *any* cattle in the middle of a dark night could result in someone getting run over and trampled to death. It happened every year, somewhere, and not just when people deliberately caused stampedes either.

When the crew left the herd out in the grass and rode in the direction of the buildings, George was waiting in the yard out front of the barn at the tie-rack. He wanted to ascertain what Jim Vargas had encountered when he'd made his last scout.

Jim looked a little abashed when he reported. "Maybe it was nothin'. Anyway, I rode back a mile, then led my horse a ways further, and never seen nothing. Never heard nothing neither." He grinned a little. "Maybe Ben and me was just getting a little spooky out there."

But George had no illusions. "We'll take turns keeping watch," he said, and turned to jerk a thumb upwards. "Better from the loft-door of the barn than from horseback. From up there a man can see hundreds of miles . . . Ben?"

Chavez said, "Sure, I'll go first." He looked at Johnny. "Does the sentry get hot coffee?"

Vargas answered. "I'll bring it up to you."

They off-saddled in the sickly, cold grey light, turned their animals out, forked down hay, then trooped over to the cookshack, with George Wayland bringing up the rear. He and Ben had talked crisply and quietly before Ben had gone up the loft-ladder and George had joined the other men.

There was very little doubt but that the free-graze men would arrive sometime today; George had a feeling it would be this morning. That is what he warned Ben Chavez about. Ben was to come on the run at the first sign of horsemen out in the dawnlight.

Cliff helped Johnny at the stove. They made up a few platters of left-overs but the men weren't hungry. They hadn't burned up very much of that earlier meal; riding out, bunching the cattle and riding back hadn't been that arduous nor that time-consuming. What they really wanted was hot coffee—hot *something*. It was cold outside.

George took his cup to the window and stood gazing out. The new day was gradually, almost reluctantly, firming up. To the south, over behind the main-house and to one side of it, was the little low, rolling rib of land where the Waylands had buried their own, including their riders, for three generations. Old Matthew was over there. George sipped bitter black coffee and his eyes puckered slightly. This was probably the first time since George had inherited, that old Matthew had actually felt warm and comfortable in his grave.

43

George's father had been more like his son than old Matthew. He too, had avoided serious trouble whenever he decently could. He must have been a terrible disappointment to old Matthew, also.

Cliff strolled to the window and looked out briefly before speaking. "You talked to 'em, George, what do you think?"

"They'll come, you can bet on that," Wayland replied, thinking of that big old rawboned, shock-headed man.

"What do you think of one of us maybe riding to town for a posse?" asked Cliff.

George, remembering his calm discussion with the town marshal, Jud Porter, answered candidly. "Jud only moves when there's been a gun fired."

Cliff Howlett also knew Constable Porter. "I could fire one under his gawddamned chair and let him chase me back here . . . Naw; I understand. I know what you mean, and you're right. Jud's a nice guy to shoot a game of pool with, but for something like *this*. . . . Want another cup of coffee?"

George turned back to the stove with Howlett. Usually, when a man devised a scheme which he knew would bring another man up out of his soogans pawing and bellowing, he had his next defensive move planned. George had thought a lot about what he had to do once the free-grazers, who outnumbered him, came boiling over to his home-place after their cattle. The trouble was that now, in quiet, undisturbed retrospect, that scheme did not seem very clever. In fact it did not even seem feasible.

He got his refill at the stove and turned back in the

direction of the window. Now, the daylight was beginning to brighten. Without even crossing the room to look out, he could see each detail of the old log barn, where Ben Chavez was hunkering in the loft, probably cold to the bones, keeping watch.

He turned and said, "Jim; take a jag of coffee over to the barn," then he turned back as Johnny Welton had a suggestion to offer.

"I can take it over, and spell Ben off."

George nodded indifferently, and Cliff reached to touch his arm. "Save it, all of you. Ben's on his way over here."

They all glanced out the window. The rangeboss was walking swiftly, hands shoved deeply into jacket pockets, in the direction of the cookshack.

"Well," muttered Howlett, "whatever's goin' to happen isn't very damned far off from happening now, gents." He fished around for his cut-plug and worried off a corner of it with big, strong white teeth.

Chavez walked in, stamped his feet and headed in a bee-line for the popping old cook-stove. "It's colder out there," he said, "than the inside of an ice-house," and having said that, he also said, "They're coming and it looks like the whole blasted band of them. They're still a couple of miles out, but they're heading straight for the cattle."

George had no chance to alter the plan he had just been viewing skeptically. "Take your carbines," he ordered, "and get strung out among the sheds and corrals. I'll ride out just beyond the edge of the yard to do the palavering." He grinned. "If it comes to shooting,

45

damn it, remember which one is me."

He led them out of the cookshack. The last man out was Ben, who had to gulp his coffee to make it, and he blew down the lamp mantle as he headed for the door. They did not need artificial light by now in any case. The sun wasn't quite up yet, and would not fully arise for some little time yet, but they had as much daylight as they would need—for whatever happened.

6

TROUBLE!

None of the men in the barn with George while he saddled a fresh horse said anything, but they clearly did not think much of his plan to ride out. If he had asked they would have suggested that he remain at the barn and let the free-grazers come to him.

He had a reason for not doing that.

When he walked forth then mounted to turn his horse, he gave them that crooked little wry smile again as he said, "Remember—I'm the one with his back to you.

They could see the oncoming horsemen easily, by now, and the free-grazers did something which was reminiscent of another variety of mounted enemy. They rode a few hundred yards, then halted for a long time to look and listen and talk a little, then they rode on again and repeated this procedure several times, the way old-time war-parties had done.

Ben, watching, grunted then said, "Get your carbines and let's get ready."

Out where George rode he could see both the free-graze men and their grazing cattle. The animals did not appear the slightest bit interested in an oncoming band of bunched-up, bristling horsemen.

George anticipated the last stop when the trespassers halted only a hundred or so yards from him, glared, then mumbled among themselves. He called out to them. "Stay away from the cattle."

The free-grazers may have had no intention of going out there to begin their own little roundup, but it was safe to assume, as George had done, that this was why they were over here.

Now, that big old shaggy-headed man with the greasy hat and the fearless, sunk-set, fanatical eyes, lifted his horse away from his companions and rode straight for George.

When he was close George said, "That's good enough. Yesterday it was your turn. Today it's my turn. The cattle stay right where they are, impounded by me. I keep them for damages or you pay for grazing across my range."

The old man leaned to expectorate, and froze as his hawk-like, intent grey eyes detected a flash of first sunlight off blue steel back among the home-place corrals. He spat, raised a soiled sleeve to mop off the residue from his chin, then eased back in the saddle with a long look at George.

"I warned you yesterday, sonny," he said harshly.

George answered quietly. "Yeah, didn't you though. Like I said: Today it's my turn. You make a move towards those cattle and they'll bury you today."

The old man considered. His predatory eyes roamed among the buildings, then swung in the direction of his own crew. The only cover was among the buildings and that was already dominated. He could test George Wayland, of course, by sending several of his boys out to the herd. If Wayland was not bluffing. . . . .

He spat again, then said, "Sonny, you need an order from a circuit rider to impound them critters. I know the law on this sort of thing."

George believed the last part of that statement. Free-grazers were forever in trouble with the law, book-law and range-law. This one would indeed know his law. But not *Wayland* law. "I've got an order to impound them," he told the older man, and lightly touched the handle of his holstered Colt. "Mister; three hundred dollars is what it's going to cost you."

"Three . . . For Chris'zake, sonny, you're as crazy as a coot."

"It'll cost me that much to trail out of the drought area and find some feed to lease," explained George. "Well; maybe not quite that much, but a man's entitled to a little pay for inconvenience isn't he?"

"Over my dead body!"

"That's not too far from happening right now," said George. "Every day you put off paying, mister, the fee goes up. The grass those cattle are on right now is part of our winter feed, and if it don't rain it's not going to grow back. Tomorrow, mister, it'll be four hundred dollars."

The old man's rugged, weathered face closed down with a flinty look of murderous finality. His eyes bored

48

into George. "You challenged the wrong feller," he said. "You just bucked a man who was bustin' heads and buryin' folks when you was still in swaddlin' clothes." He started to raise a big balled fist.

George's draw was fast. He rested the barrel upon the saddle-swells. All he had ever meant to do was lay down his range-law in a civil tone. He had never believed that would end it, and he had never for a moment, after their previous meeting, believed this old devil would yield. Now he spoke to the free-grazer in a harsher tone.

"Listen, you old son of a bitch, I don't give a damn who you are or what you've done. You raise that arm to signal, and I'm going to kill you." He paused, held the older man's stare without blinking, and when the free-grazer rested that balled fist upon the saddletop, George did not put up his weapon, he gestured with it.

"Dismount!"

The old man glared. "The hell I will."

George eased back the hammer and tilted the barrel a notch. *"Dismount!"*

They sat glaring. This was supposed to be a palaver, a talk between hostile rangemen to determine which one could run the best bluff or count the first coup, but it was not supposed to end in gunfire. Even if either of them had thought those ugly Texas cattle were worth being killed over, there was protocol.

George's trigger-finger whitened slightly at the knuckle and the older man saw this. He reddened to a rusty, splotchy color and swung his right leg loose of the cantle to come down upon the left side of his animal.

"Shed the Colt," George said.

The old man ran reins through his fingers popping them a couple of times. He was being humiliated; not beaten, because you couldn't beat a man who was not defeatable, but to his kind of a person humiliation was someone's death warrant. He had wanted to kill someone this badly before in his lifetime, and generally he had been able to do it. Not now; he had badly misjudged this youthful cowman. Badly misjudged the temperament of a rangeman, something he had not done in a long time.

"I don't shed my gun for no man," he snarled, and George saw the tentative look in those fierce grey eyes. George did not answer, he simply moved his gunbarrel slightly to track the dismounted man.

"No. Wait," said the older man, and lifted out his Colt to let it fall. He was savagely, icily angry. He would have jumped George bare-handed if he had dared.

"What do you figure this is going to accomplish?" he demanded of the younger man. "You see them boys out yonder?

George ignored these remarks and gestured. "Walk back towards that log barn. I'll tell you what this is going to accomplish. You are going to get shot or hanged, one or the other, that's what's going to happen at the first move one of those men make. Mister; you never been as close to a burying as you are right now. Start walking!"

George turned his horse, leaned to wrench the reins

away from the older man and swear. "Damn it, I said *walk!*"

The free-graze man walked woodenly and without looking left or right. He was tall and rough-built and oaken, and he was also deadly wrathful. There was no room for self-reproach; he had never in his life had room for that in his rages, but he acknowledged as he hiked along that he had made an almost disastrous mistake in a man. Maybe it was a disastrous mistake, not just "almost" one.

Ben Chavez stood up slowly, carbine held crossways, watchful of the other free-graze men, but they were sitting out there like stone images not even talking among themselves as they watched their spokesman being herded along. They had been unable to see the pistol until their spokesman had dismounted, and by then it was too late; they could have shot George, in all probability, and if they had tried it he or someone over among those corrals and sheds would have shot the old man.

Chavez stepped out into plain sight when George herded the captive up to him. Ben was tall, but he had to raise his eyes to the craggy, unshaven, villainous-looking rusty-red face of the big old free-graze man.

George said, "In the barn, Ben. I'm not through yet." He started to rein around when the older man snarled at him.

"You're through. Mark my words you're through!"

Ben snarled and rammed his Winchester barrel, hard, so hard the old man gasped in spite of himself. He then continued his march in the direction of the barn with

Ben Chavez behind him.

George holstered his Colt, glanced out where those other free-grazers were still sitting their saddles, and reined off in that direction.

But he halted mid-way and let the reins hang. He had no intention of going close enough to have the same thing happen to him.

"You'll get the old bastard back," he called to the band of bristling rangeriders, "when I've been paid for my grass. Three hundred dollars if it's paid today, four hundred if it's paid tomorrow. If it's not paid by day after tomorrow I will claim the cattle and re-brand them."

A younger rawboned, large, rough-looking rider urged his mount out a few feet and glared. "You ain't going to get a damned thing but a bullet in the back of the head. You think we're goin' to be robbed by you, or any other damned land-hog? You think wrong!"

He whirled, bawled a profane order, and led the entire band of horsemen back westerly. When they were strung out, George and his watching men could count them. Without the older man there were seven of them. There should have been nine all told, or, without the older man, there should have been eight of them.

George turned back, rode into the yard, stepped off out front of the barn and did not return the broad smile of Johnny Welton when he came forward to take charge of the saddle-horse.

In the barn that old man looked for all the world like an old, war-wise lobo wolf surrounded by smaller but equally as deadly hounds. He stood wide-legged in his full-fledged defiance. When George walked in, loosened his jacket and thumbed back his hat, the old man said, "They'll draw and quarter you for this. When they get organized, damn you anyway, they'll come back here and set a torch to every damned thing you own; when they're through you'll be nothing but a patch of jelly out there in that damned yard!"

Cliff Howlett gazed dispassionately upon the older man. "What the hell is your name?" he asked. "You sound like a warped old crazy preacher I heard one time over at Fort Sumpter."

The free-grazer glared only at George, and that annoyed Cliff who stepped up to rap the old man's arm and make his demand over again. The old man swung like a striking snake. Cliff had no chance to avoid all the blow, but he, too, was very fast; he swiveled from the hips and the sledging blow staggered him as it bounced off his turning body.

George moved in quickly. Cliff had a bad temper and the older man was unarmed. George stepped between them as Jim Vargas leaned and gave their captive a hard shove which nearly spilled the old man, but when he recovered and whirled, Jim had a knife-blade turned sideways, poised. Jim was grinning.

Cliff was white to the eyes but he said nothing. He massaged his sore ribs and turned his back to walk up to the front of the barn and stand out there until the fury in his heart subsided.

George faced the old man. "He asked you a fair question. What *is* your name?"

"Hiram Rockwell, and you'll not forget it as long as

53

you live!" snarled the old man. "Lots of folks know my name, mister, and a lot more of 'em only heard it once—that was a second before they died."

George looked from Ben to Johnny to Jim. Cliff was still standing up in the doorway with his back to them all. Ben was not very impressed by the defiant, fierce old free-graze man. "I'll get some chains from the blacksmith shop and lock him to one of the barn-baulks," he said, "and when *they* come sneakin' in here tonight to free him, Jim and I'll be waiting."

Hiram Rockwell watched the rangeboss hike out of the barn and across the sunbright yard. "You listen to a damn In'ian," he spat at George. "You hired filthy damned heathen?"

George looked at Jim, and winked. Jim winked back and neither of them said a word.

7

A BEAUTIFUL NIGHT

Cliff's wrath was gone but his ribs still pained him, so when Ben said he'd chained the old man to one of the barn-baulks Cliff mentioned how he would like it if the old devil would break loose while he was over there guarding him.

Johnny said, "Cliff, that looked like a mule kicking."

Howlett answered affirmatively. "Felt like it, too. For an old man, that mangy old cuss has the strength of a grizzly—"

Vargas had climbed to the loft to see if there was still

any sign of the other free-grazers. He returned to report that he could not see them, so they must have gone all the way back to their wagon, which was a long way westerly in the direction of Blue Sump.

"They'll make a try for the old bastard tonight sure as hell," said Johnny Welton.

Ben was rolling a smoke and commented without raising his head "I'll be out there, waiting. Jim will spell me off." He flicked the paper, lipped the cigarette and struck a match. "They couldn't get him loose even if none of us was out there. I chained him with bolts instead of locks. I riveted each bolt. *I* can't even get him loose." Ben inhaled, exhaled, and said, "I done it that way for a reason. He said something about burning us out. Well; if they come with torches and fire the barn you know who's going up with it, don't you?"

George had something to say that made them all stare. "Good, Ben. That's exactly what we need. For Rockwell to be chained so's he can't get loose even if he had a file to work with all night long. Because we aren't going to be here when his friends show up. *If* they show up." He turned. "Johnny, go pitch a horseblanket over that old devil. Don't say a word to him, just give him something to keep warm with, then start fetching in horses. . . . We're going to hunt up their wagon tonight."

For a moment no one moved. Johnny Welton left them, finally, heading across in the direction of the barn. It was still mid-afternoon with golden sunlight covering everything. The far-away hills were shimmery from a bluish heat-haze. The sky, as usual, was pale and cloudless.

Cliff said, "Shouldn't one of us stay here, just in case?"

George looked at Ben. "You sure he can't get loose, and no one can file him loose?"

Ben was sure. "He'll be there. Unless they cut off both feet and one hand, then pull the stumps out of the chains. All the same I'll drag over more chain. I didn't know you figured on us not being here tonight . . . George, suppose they fire the main-house or the cook-shack or the bunkhouse, and not the barn?"

Cliff passed that over. "Not likely; and have sparks settle on the roof and burn the barn with the old man in it? By the way, he don't *pay* eight riders does he? He don't have that big a herd, and whoever heard of one of those bastards paying anybody."

Johnny returned round-eyed. "You know, that old devil can do something I admire in a man. He can cuss for a straight fact and never repeat none of it, and do it for a full three minutes. Now that takes talent!" Johnny waited for the murmurs of admiration which did not come, then he said, "When I brought in fresh horses and tied them, Rockwell said if we ride out, his lads'll be out there hiding and they'll pot-shoot us like we was prairie chickens. I asked him where will they hide in a country that hasn't had any rain for two years."

George stepped over and glanced at the position of the sun. They still had several hours of daylight. This time of year full darkness did not arrive until almost ten o'clock at night. He had no intention of riding out before full darkness. Whether they could find hiding places or not, Rockwell's riders would certainly be keeping an intent watch on the Wayland home-place. George had his own idea about what he and his men were going to do. It did not include being spied out and perhaps trailed by any of the free-graze men.

They went over to the cookshack, had a leisurely meal which was too late for dinner and too early for supper, then George left the others and went down to the barn where old Rockwell was sitting upon the blanket Johnny had tossed to him.

The old man glared, then tried to turn away so he would not have to look at Wayland. The chains prevented him from accomplishing his purpose, and George simply stepped around until they faced one another. The older man was venomous.

"If I never do anything else, I'm going to kill you, Wayland, and turn this ranch of yours back to nature. When I'm finished there won't be a stick of wood nor a—"

"You should have been a preacher," stated George, and fished out his makings. "Care for a smoke?"

"From you the only thing I'd accept," snapped the old man, "would be blood. All you've got!"

George rolled the cigarette and lit it, then he leaned on the nearby wall gauging his prisoner. "The girl wasn't with them today. Why not?"

Hiram Rockwell sat like an old strong-heart buck, glaring fiercely past his tormentor unwilling to say a word.

George blew smoke. "We're going over there as soon as it gets dark, Mister Rockwell, and fetch her back here."

That brought the older man's head up. "They'll catch you and kill every man-jack of you!"

George was not perturbed. "I figure they'll be coming over here, creeping around for an hour or so first to be sure they won't get shot, before they sneak into the barn to free you. . . . My rangeboss is bringing over more chains. We don't figure they're going to get you free unless they cut off a foot or a hand. Meanwhile, we're going after the girl."

"Wayland, you damned . . . !"

"Mister Rockwell, what is she to you? Your daughter?"

"I'll strangle you bare-handed the minute I get these chains off me, Wayland. I promise you! I give you my word!"

"Your niece then. She's too young to be your wife."

"My wife died in Missouri years ago, starved and broken and beaten down by land-hogs like you, Wayland, and ever since I've taken my share of their treasure, by gawd. An eye for an eye!"

George dropped the smoke and stepped on it, and afterwards continued to gaze downward. It was cooler inside the barn than it was out in the yard, but it was still uncomfortable. George went over to the bunkhouse for the *olla* and returned with it. As he leaned to set it gently beside Hiram Rockwell he said, "If we get the girl, there is still going to be trouble. You've caused it, but still, I hope none of your crew gets killed. Drink the water; we'll feed you just before we pull out tonight." George stood gazing down. "She's your daughter, isn't she?"

58

Rockwell lifted the *olla* to tilt it and drink. When his eyes met those of George Wayland he said, "She is my daughter, and four of them men is my sons. The other three are hyenas, jackals, but they work for what they eat and drink and I need 'em for the cattle. . . . Wayland; any one of those three can cut your throat in your own bed without disturbin' the dust."

Rockwell drank deeply, set the earthenware *olla* gently upon the hardpacked groundfloor of the barn, and sighed. Sweat started out under his shirt immediately. "Leave it be," he mumbled in a dull tone. "I'll drift on out of the country and that'll end it. Leave it be and don't make it no worse for all of us. I'm willing, Wayland."

George said, "But I'm not willing. Three hundred dollars today, four hundred tomorrow, and the day after I'm going to claim the cattle and re-brand them. Mister Rockwell . . . day after tomorrow I may also bury one or two of your sons. Maybe the girl. It will be up to you."

He walked out of the barn and looked to the north. There was a strange, opaque murkiness over there, more than heat-haze, more than dust-banners, more even than the filtering-down shadows of evening. He was transfixed by it and stood there staring until Johnny called from the cookshack porch.

"Got fresh coffee."

They ignored the old man when they finally went to the barn to saddle up. They did not speak to him nor talk among themselves. They were walking their horses into the yard in the darkness when Hiram Rockwell called George back.

He said, "I been thinkin'. You're going to get some men killed."

George interrupted. "*I'm* not going to get anyone killed. *I* didn't bring a herd of free-graze damned cattle into a drought country and try to ruin any cowmen. *You* did those things. *You're* the one who is going to—"

"Let me finish, damn you," snarled the old man, suddenly angry. "I told you—I been thinkin'. All right; you done something blessed few folks ever been able to do, you beat Hiram Rockwell. Of course you done it underhanded; I came over just to palaver with you, and you threw down on me."

George started back out of the barn. He had heard all this before.

"Wait!" commanded the old man. "Listen to me. I said I been thinkin' and I have. I'll pull out tomorrow; have my cattle and riders off your range by tomorrow evenin'. That's fair, Mister Wayland."

George faced around. First, it had been "sonny" then it had been "Wayland" and now it was "*Mister* Wayland." Rockwell learned respect the hard way. He had to be in chains sitting in the dirt before it came to him.

George said, "You know blamed well that's only part of the terms. Three hundred dollars, and I've got to have it in my hand before midnight, otherwise it becomes four hundred—or the cattle."

"You'll never get the cattle," flared the older man, glaring in the darkness. "They'll stampede them back to our camp, and you can bet new money on that!"

George answered mildly. Too mildly. "Mister Rockwell, I figured that. I thought your boys were probably plenty experienced at stealing cattle in the darkness. And I don't have enough men to prevent it, do I? But your daughter will make a better hostage anyway; she won't eat too much, and we'll be around here waiting, when your men try to get *her* back. . . . Do you have anything else to say? If not we're wasting time."

The old man may have had to learn how bitter captivity was but he still was not defeated. He had a powerful will, obviously, or he never would have come this far through life against great odds and powerful adversaries, and it was this will, this blind-stubbornness, which made him flare out again when he said, "They'll kill you. I'll see to it myself!"

George turned and walked out of the barn.

The night was warm, the stars were pegged in place, the men mounted and followed George at a walk out of the yard. He did not say a word until they had covered almost a mile then he halted and for a moment they all sat listening before he said, "Ben, can you and Jim find their camp, grab the girl and bring her back?"

The men stared. Ben said he and Vargas could probably do that; what did George have in mind?

"I'd like to be in the loft when they come for the old man," he explained. "And just in case they *can* get the old bastard loose, some of us should be there to prevent them from firing the buildings. Mainly, I want to hear what they talk about."

"They'll talk about us grabbin' the girl," stated Cliff, matter-of-factly. "The old man'll tell 'em, and they'll bust back the way they come, lookin' for us and her."

Chavez agreed. "Yeah. If she's his daughter he'll be fit to be tied thinkin' of us grabbing her. He'll send them back fast."

"Only you won't come directly back here, will you?" said George. "You can go northward or southward and follow a different trail."

Ben didn't need that kind of a comment. "Don't you worry about Jim and me," he told George. "They won't get us. But if they suspicion you fellers are in the loft or close by . . . remember, there are eight or nine of them."

George was not likely to forget. He smiled at Ben. "Good luck. We'll be keeping watch for you come dawn."

Chavez and Jim Vargas turned and loped westerly. They did not know where the free-graze camp was, but if anyone could find it in the darkness they could.

George turned back, but now he led the two riders accompanying him a mile southward. The perils of his current undertaking were many, but the first and foremost peril was detection; if they were caught and cornered by Hiram Rockwell's riders. . . .

Cliff said, "Nice night," and both his companions stared at him. Cliff shrugged. It *was* a nice night; in fact it was a beautiful night. If people like Rockwell and his riding crew also made it a deadly and hazardous night that didn't change a damned thing about the night itself. Cliff was right, it was a magnificent night.

8

THE BATTLE!

They off-saddled, removed the bridles and released their saddle animals a half mile out, over near the round hilltop where the Wayland Ranch cemetery was. They left their riding gear inside the old iron fence behind several large old trees, then they sat down to remove their spurs, arose with only their carbines in hand, and began the quiet stalk back in the direction of the barn.

There were two ways into the loft; there were short scantlings nailed to the backwall, outside, which led upwards to the loft door, and there was the interior set of steps going up the north wall to a trapdoor in the loft floor.

When they got near the barn with George leading, his intention to use the back-wall ladder, Johnny Welton said, "Hold it; I think I hear something."

They halted to listen mid-way between the bunkhouse and the log barn. The sound which Johnny had heard and which was still audible, was the muted, distant, almost imperceptible whisper of cattle moving.

Cliff said, "By gawd they're *easing* their damned cattle away. I figured sure as hell they'd bust them out in a stampede."

"They're good hands, no question about that," murmured George, but it wasn't the loss of the cattle which held him still and thoughtful. If the free-graze riders had decided to reclaim their cattle, then they must not have had in mind trying to release Hiram Rockwell. They surely wouldn't believe they could accomplish both the same night. He jerked his head and led off. They covered the final few yards and this time it was George who flung up an arm to halt their stealthy approach.

He whispered. "Voices. You hear them? Inside the barn."

It was hard to hear the voices because they were not only low and subdued, but they had lapses between sentences. George crept to the barn's backwall, pulling loose the tie-down of his Colt as he slid forward. What he wanted to hear was the words; he wanted to know the plans of the free-graze men. He wanted to hear the reaction of the younger ones when that old devil in chains told his boys and his riders Wayland's crew was on its way to abduct the girl.

What he eventually heard was a fierce snarl from farther back where Cliff Howlett was, and when George turned he saw them rushing out of the darkness, three of them with carbines. Who they were and how they had managed to detect the Wayland-crew was something George would not have the time to reflect upon. One of those men shouted. "Andy! Out the back, quick!"

Cliff Howlett went down under the savage clubbing of a pair of Winchesters and Johnny Welton, reaching for his holster, was slammed savagely against the log wall by a swung carbine. Johnny wilted but only momentarily, then he tried to duck low to avoid the second blow, and George sprang at the man with the hauled-back Winchester, caught him around the neck and wrenched him viciously backwards. The man stumbled and tried to make a noise but the powerful arm around his neck and against his voice-box cut him off from uttering a sound. The man struggled, but he had made a bad mistake, he had not looked to see if there was anyone beyond Johnny. Now, George whirled the man and swung with perfect timing. His blow snapped the man's head back so hard it struck the log wall. The free-graze man dropped his carbine and toppled forward off the barnwall.

Johnny had an injured gun-arm, but he swore and catapulted himself at one of the men who had clubbed down Cliff Howlett. George sprang over the man he had knocked senseless to join Johnny. They bracketed one of the men standing over Cliff.

When this free-grazer turned to face Johnny, who was closest, he had George on his blind side, and George, with a third free-grazer suddenly twisting to face the threat of a pair of Wayland-riders, had no time. He drew his Colt and swung it overhand. The blow drove the stranger's hat past his ears. The man's knees jackknifed and he fell into Johnny, who flailed away with his good arm and fist.

That third free-graze man had his carbine half raised, had his thumb on the hammer when George pushed the Colt straight at the man. Neither of them moved a muscle.

A lanky youth with curly hair spilling from beneath a dirty old disreputable hat, appeared from inside the barn with a sixgun in his hand, low and uncocked. He saw the Mexican stand-off and started to raise his pistol to break it. He evidently had not seen Johnny Welton, but when he raised that gun Johnny said, "Freeze, you son of a bitch or I'll blow your damned head off!"

No one could possibly have misinterpreted Johnny's sincerity. The big youth froze; he did not complete the raising of his gun and he did not turn his head in Johnny's direction.

"Drop 'em," ordered Johnny, addressing both the free-graze men. "Gawddamn you I said *drop 'em!*"

Johnny cocked his handgun. The big youth let his gun fall first. The man facing George with the carbine, slowly came up out of his gunfighting crouch. He eased up his grip and dropped the Winchester.

Cliff Howlett groaned from underfoot. No one paid him the slightest attention. George still had the murky look in his eyes of a man fully willing to kill, to fight, when he stepped from between the two unarmed men and Johnny herded the big youth over beside the other man. From inside the barn old Rockwell's unmistakable harsh voice bawled out.

"Andy; you got 'em? Is one of 'em Wayland? Boy come in here and get me out of these chains. I got a score to settle with Wayland."

George motioned with his Colt for the pair of captives to turn and face the barn wall. He stepped in close to go over them for a belly-gun or a bootknife. Behind him Johnny was massaging his aching right arm and working it to ascertain if there was anything broken. There wasn't, but the upper-arm muscle was in a large, hard knot and the pain seemed to emanate from this bad bruise.

Johnny went over to help Cliff to his feet. Howlett had blood on the side of his cheek. It had trickled from a scalp wound. As soon as he felt the blood and saw it on his hand, Cliff affected an almost miraculous recovery. He turned, still holding the bloody hand aloft, and looked at the nearest free-graze man who was facing the barn wall. It was not the youth, it was the other, shorter and older and more oaken man. Without a word of warning Cliff stepped in, caught that man with a grip on his shoulder using the left hand, spun the free-graze man around and fired from as high as the shoulder with his blood-spattered right hand. The blow made a sound as though it were a distant pistol-shot. The rangerider bounced off the log wall and collapsed. Blood ran from his smashed mouth after he was down and sprawling.

The youth twisted and raised both arms to protect himself, believing Cliff would step over the fallen man and go after him. Cliff stopped, opened and closed his right hand a few times, then turned away.

George looked around. It looked like a battlefield with unconscious men lying underfoot and weapons scattered in all directions. He told the youth to put his arms down, then he said, "Are you Andy?"

The youth nodded.

"Who else was in the barn with you, Andy?"

The youth answered sullenly, gazing at the bloody faced man at his feet. "No one. It was just me."

"You and your paw?"

"Yes."

George gestured. "Lend a hand and we'll drag this carrion inside for your paw to see. Then we'll lynch 'em." George's gun was pointed squarely at the big youth's middle. Andy looked, not at the menacing gun, but at George's face.

"Lynch 'em?"

George's reply was curt. "Do as I tell you; grab a pair of boots and let's drag them inside."

Johnny and Cliff moved in to help but neither of them was in very good condition, so it required both men to drag one of the downed free-graze riders, whereas Andy could do it by himself, and George stood a little to one side with his Colt aimed at the big youth. But Andy did not seem to have any defiance left in him. He had good reason not to have; without there actually being much chance for them to come out of this on top, the Wayland-riders had done exactly that.

The three men who had had the advantage of surprise were unconscious, battered, disarmed and bloody. The three men who had been surprised and had had *no* advantage, were now the victors.

Old Hiram Rockwell twisted as far as he could in his chains trying to make out who was entering the rear of the barn, and who was being dragged inside, but the darkness was too intent so he had to content himself with growling questions which no one answered.

George pointed and the inert free-graze men were dragged over in front of old Rockwell and unceremoniously dumped there. His big son, Andy, was shoved over there too, by Cliff Howlett, who was in no frame

68

of mind to be gentle.

Cliff faced the big youth, gun dangling from his right side. "Who else is in the yard?"

Andy answered in the same deep, sullen tone of voice again. "No one. Everyone else is out with the cattle."

"Are they likely to come over here?"

"No. They was to just pick up the cattle and keep 'em moving. We was to do what had to be done over here." Andy studied George. "You'll be Mister Wayland?"

"Yeah."

"Well; my paw said you and your crew went after Sandy."

"Sandy?"

"My sister, Samantha. Paw said—"

Hiram Rockwell spoke harshly. "There's more of 'em. Andy, there's them two In'ians Wayland's got riding for him, and they aren't here . . . Gawddamn you, Wayland, if you sent bloodthirsty savages after my girl—"

"That's exactly who I sent," growled George, and leaned to shove the barrel of his gun against the old man's chest. "The trouble with folks who set out to start trouble, a lot of the time Mister Rockwell, is that they don't know how the folks they antagonize fight."

Johnny Welton, cradling his painful right arm, said, "Safe to light the lantern, George?"

Cliff had the thing in his hand. One side of his head was matted with blood but he did not *act* as badly injured as he *looked.* When George conceded, Cliff lighted the lantern and suspended it from its overhead peg, then went out back to gather up weapons back there where the fierce little battle had taken place. During his absence George and Johnny gazed upon the lighted face of the men they had battered senseless. One of them was moving and the other two seemed to want to groan, to clear their throats or something like that because they made noises in their throats.

George turned on Andy. "Are they your brothers?"

Andy woodenly nodded, and Cliff, entering the barn from out back in time to see Andy's nod, dumped the guns he had found against the wall and said, "George; we got the whole blessed family except the girl, by gawd."

"We'll have her, come dawn," stated Johnny, then, looking deliberately venomous, he said, "Unless of course them In'ians decide to cut her throat. They get roiled up real easy if prisoners yell or fight or try and break free. Some of the stories I've heard about what them savages did to folks. . . ."

"Get a bucket of water," said George, "and sluice off these other Rockwells, Johnny."

Cliff stepped up and leaned to look down into the wide-open eyes of the man he had knocked senseless. Cliff made a little clucking sound then extended a hand to help the Rockwell rider to his feet. As he was steadying this man Cliff said, "You got awful hard teeth, mister, I cut two knuckles on 'em."

Johnny came back and used both his arms, even the painful one, to up-end the waterbucket. Both the downed men gasped and floundered, then tried to scramble away and slipped back in the mud.

George holstered his Colt. Hiram Rockwell was

staring at George. He did not say a word and his face for once did not have that stubbornly malevolent glare to it.

George returned the older man's look briefly, then sent Johnny after all the chain he could locate over in both the blacksmith shop and the wagon-shed. He and his men had been outnumbered right from the start of their difficulty with the free-graze riders, and they were still outnumbered by them, especially in the barn at the ranch, but once they had all those Rockwells in chains, the matter of odds would be changed considerably, and that was what George wanted to see happen.

He rolled and lit a smoke and watched his two riders working with the chains Johnny brought back. Not a word was said by the prisoners or their captors as each man was literally weighted down with chairs, and securely riveted into them.

It hadn't been a bad night's work at all.

9

FACE TO FACE

Before morning Cliff's head was swollen and his ribs which still ached from the time when old Rockwell had caught him off-guard, pained him even more as the result of being struck several times alongside the body by those carbine-swinging Rockwells.

Johnny's right arm lost some of its swelling, but the pain was greater now that it was centralized. Only George had come through the fight last night without injury, so he did most of the hauling when they went over to the little cemetery-hill for their saddles and bridles.

Later, when they went across to the cookshack to make coffee and a meal, George went to the main-house and returned with a bottle of rye whisky. Cliff and Johnny laced their hot coffee with that, and their subsequent recovery was considerably expedited. None of them offered to take coffee out to those filthy, soggy, battered men chained to the barn-baulks. They all probably thought of it but none of them mentioned it. They were vastly more concerned with the Chavez-Vargas mission, but actually they had worlds of faith in the rangeboss and beefy, squatty Jim Vargas. It was the unpredictable, the unexpected, that worried them.

They knew for a fact that Chavez and Vargas would be killed on sight if those remaining free-graze men accidentally located them and found that they had Samantha Rockwell with them.

"It won't happen," scoffed Cliff. "You couldn't no more accidentally ride down a couple of desert Indians than you could fly from here to San Francisco. You won't never be able to do neither of those things." Cliff pushed his cup forward to be refilled with rye whisky and coffee. "They'll be along directly. My guess is that they'll take a damned long way around gettin' back to the ranch. That'll waste maybe two, three more hours, but they'll be along."

George had the same confidence, but he was also mindful of the inadvertencies even though he did not mention them. He glanced out the window several times, then watched Johnny Welton rub his sore, bruised and discolored upper right arm with liniment. The cookshack acquired the smell of that liniment, which was a composite of several heating chemicals none of which had been included in the concoction because of its aroma.

Cliff accepted the bottle with a wrinkled brow when Johnny was finished with it. Cliff read the instructions on the bottle's reverse side and decided he did not have any of the ailments the liniment was supposed to alleviate and pushed it away as he arose to refill his cup for the third time. *This* was the kind of medicine Cliff Howlett appreciated.

They did, eventually, take some coffee out to the barn. By then it was turning chilly and dawn was not far off. The Rockwells were sitting in rumpled, soiled gloom. They had talked sporadically but they were not speaking when George Wayland and his riders entered the barn. Each one of them accepted a cup of black coffee, and when they tasted it, found it to be liberally laced with whisky, they looked a little less sullen. It was the old man who broke the silence by saying, "We're obliged. It don't change a single thing, you understand, but we're obliged."

"Sure," said Cliff, sarcastically, "and now tell us you'd do as much for us, you old bastard."

Hiram looked steadily at Cliff. "I'll settle with you for calling me that, when I'm out of these chains," he said.

Cliff looked unimpressed as he turned from Hiram to the man Cliff had smashed in the mouth. "You too," he said. "You'll want a piece of my hide too, I figure. Well;

73

whenever you're ready." He walked past and looked out into the westerly darkness. Cliff was one of those men who made as everlasting an enemy as he made an everlasting friend.

One of the battered men in the soggy clothes said, "Mister Wayland, we'll see that you get three hundred dollars," and George looked from the speaker to the other sons of Hiram Rockwell. Before he, or they, could speak, Hiram cursed the son who had spoken, raged at him and accused him of betraying his own father. The younger man sat through all that unflinching, and when Hiram had to pause for breath his son said, "From one gawddamnęd danger to another ever since I can remember, paw, and no more for me. He gets his three hundred dollars."

"A bullet is all he'll ever get from the Rockwells!" exclaimed the old man, and raised a clenched fist with a chain encircling its wrist. "You eat my food and ride my horses and—"

"And work like a slave, and do things for you that turn my stomach," snarled the younger man, "and for what? One-fifth share of a herd of mangy Texas cattle that if you sold them tomorrow wouldn't fetch me what I'd get in honest wages from any cow outfit in six months' time." The son glared at his father, then turned his head away in disgust.

Hiram glared around. "I'd thrash you 'thin an inch of your life if I was free of these chains, boy. I'd teach you what for! Making a spectacle of us all before strangers, by gawd!"

George said, "Drink your coffee, Mister Rockwell

and shut your damned mouth."

"Don't you tell me what to do!" raged the old man. Cliff turned from the rear barn opening. "George, if you and Johnny'd go over to the bunkhouse for a minute." Cliff was gazing steadily at Hiram Rockwell. He did not say more and he did not look particularly venomous, but none of them failed to understand what he had in mind. Even old Rockwell understood, because he turned quickly to George.

"That's murder and you know it, Mister Wayland. If you fellers walk out and leave us here with that man, it'll be murder pure and simple."

Cliff turned back to looking out into the darkness again. He had made his offer and George had done nothing about accepting it. As far as Cliff was concerned that old devil should have been hanged or shot, then discreetly buried before sunrise.

Johnny rolled and lit a smoke, and when one of the soggy, demoralized men on the wet earthen floor watched him do this, Johnny leaned and shoved the cigarette into the man's mouth, then flicked a match for it. Without a word he then rolled another smoke, and he did it largely one-handed because of the pain in his right arm. When the man in chains had sucked back a big lungful of smoke, then trickled it out, he eyed Johnny without real animus, and said, "Thanks. Some things make the world look right even when you're chained to a log and are settin' in muddy water on a damned barn floor." The prisoner almost smiled. "A drink of laced java and a smoke."

Johnny was encouraged by this quiet, conversational

statement and tried a question. "Where you fellers come from?"

Hiram glared. "Don't you answer that," he exclaimed, but the man with the cigarette drooping from his lips only glanced briefly at the old man before speaking.

"Texas, originally, but hell, we been grazing cattle all over. New Mexico, Arizona, Utah, Colorado, you name it, mister, and we been there grazing 'em on through until they was slick, then trailing them to a rails-end somewhere and shipping them off to Chicago. Mister, it's a hard life."

George studied the sons of Hiram Rockwell. It was on the tip of his tongue to tell them that they were as old as he was; there was no law under the sun that said they had to ride with their father, making a new set of enemies every day of their lives. The reason he said nothing was because those men, even big Andy, who most nearly resembled the old man in size and heft and coloring, and who was the youngest of the lot, was no child; every one of them knew perfectly well he did not have to do what he had been doing.

George watched Cliff turn back from studying the yonder night, and remove his plug to whittle off a corner. For the first time Hiram Rockwell's defiant and hostile eyes looked different. He watched Cliff's big knife worry off that piece of sweet plug-tobacco with the look of a drowning man first sighting dry land.

Cliff also saw the look. There was a faint glow of pre-dawn silver-grey inside the barn by this time. Dawn was closer. Any minute now it would begin its painfully slow process of birthing a fresh new day.

Cliff pouched his chew and stood there, big knife in one hand, cut-plug in the other hand, his swollen face and blood-matted hair giving him an indescribably evil look.

For a long moment this private tableau between two men who were addicted to the bitter-sweet, tangy good flavor of chewing tobacco excluded everything else.

George watched too; he knew Cliff Howlett; he was not a man who forgave easily; he had plenty of reason to sneer at the old man sitting in chains on the barn floor. George had just about made up his mind this was what was going to happen, when Cliff raised his right hand with the big-bladed knife in it, flicked his wrist and the knife spun through the air to land tip-first in the earth in front of Hiram Rockwell. Then Cliff pitched over the plug. Hiram caught it one-handed and started to speak; at least he looked as though he would say something appreciative, but Cliff turned on his heel and walked out through the rear barn opening in the direction of the working corrals.

One minute later he called from out there. "George; riders comin'."

It was the sound, not the sighting, which had alerted Cliff. He waited by the corrals until his associates from within the barn walked out to him, then he pointed in the correct direction and cupped his other hand around one ear.

It sounded like no more than perhaps three riders. At least that was George's impression, but then he and the other two rangemen *wanted* it to be three riders.

There was also the possibility that it could be those other free-graze men, the ones Hiram Rockwell had described as hyenas and jackals. By now they surely would have guessed that something had gone wrong with the rescue attempt back at the Wayland barn.

It was possible that they were returning to satisfy their curiosity or their misgivings. Cliff thought so, after listening for a long while to the oncoming sounds, but Johnny Welton said, "Hell no; if they're just half as *coyote* as the old man said they were, they wouldn't be riding in close enough to be heard."

There were arguments against that contention, too, but no one offered them. George finally loosened the Colt in his hip-holster and started walking ahead, northward. He went as far as the last of the circular working-corrals. Out there, the three of them stood and listened again.

It wasn't free-graze men, George would have bet money on that. His hopes were already rising even before a little prairie wolf barked insistently, then paused and yapped more insistently the second time.

Cliff cupped both hands and attempted a reply. Johnny groaned and rolled up his eyes, and somewhere out in the near distance a man's hearty laugh came echoing.

Cliff grinned and shrugged. Not everyone was good at this sort of thing.

Jim Vargas came first, saddlegun balanced across his lap. Next came Ben Chavez with his lariat around the gullet of a fine-looking chestnut horse with a flaxen mane and tail. All they could see of Samantha

Rockwell was that she was wearing a split riding skirt and a pale-tanned buckskin jacket with a scarf loosely tied around her throat. She wore no hat and her dark hair was worn close and curly. She was not short; in fact she was taller than Jim Vargas, but not taller than Ben Chavez.

She entered the yard, eyed the men on the ground particularly George Wayland, and showed scorn on her handsome face which was clear to the men even in the poor light.

George gestured in the direction of the cookshack, so Jim and Ben rode over there. For the time being George did not want the girl to talk to her father or her brothers. Also, she and her escort should be hungry.

As soon as they tied up over there and swung off, Ben got a good look at Cliff and Johnny. He looked all around, then said, "What happened to you fellers?"

Before either of the injured men could comment George suggested they all go inside where it was warmer and where they could get some hot coffee.

Johnny turned up the lamp then they all stood a moment gazing at Sandy Rockwell. Along with being tall, she was also a full woman in every way that counted, and handsome. Not beautiful in the sense that women who had led sheltered existences were beautiful, but handsome in a clean, wholesome, physically vibrant and strong, sense. She looked defiantly back and did not make a sound but when her glance swung to George Wayland again, there was obvious antagonism and challenge in it.

George had only seen her at a distance, before, and

that had been when she'd been bent low over a rifle. In the lamplight of his cookshack she didn't look the same. He was impressed with her and she hadn't even spoken to him yet.

10

THE ANGRY CAPTIVE

Ben Chavez stood with a cup in one hand eyeing their female prisoner when he dryly said, "George, don't turn your back on her. She hates your guts and she's never even spoken to you." Ben looked squarely at the woman and she looked unflinchingly back. "Give her half a chance and she'll try to grab your gun."

Johnny Welton offered to lace her black coffee and she yanked back the cup and glared. Johnny reddened slightly and turned away. He had only been trying to be friendly.

George was deliberately silent. He let the others talk and from time to time he would look at the girl. She did not, initially, seem impressed by Wayland, but the longer she sat there watching, the more she became curious about him—and his silence. Finally, she scarcely watched the others at all, not even when Cliff asked about the other free-graze men, and Jim said he and Ben had heard them moving the cattle, but he and Ben had been more than a mile northward where they could have whipped up into the foothills at the first sign of trouble.

"They was being awful quiet," stated Vargas. "It's not

how we figured they'd do it, there being so many of them."

The answer to that, of course, was that *there hadn't* been so many of them, and Cliff explained that all the Rockwells had been in the yard tonight, and that now they were all in chains, which left the roundup and drive to be completed by the remaining free-graze men, whose original plan had evidently been to steal back their cattle as quietly and discreetly as possible.

When Sandy Rockwell heard this she spoke to George for the first time. "You have my father and brothers?"

He answered curtly, "Yes, and now it's too light to hang them so we'll have to wait until tonight."

She stared and because she could not make up her mind about George, she believed what he had said. His riders listened, then went indifferently back to their coffee and their discussion. Cliff and Johnny, exhibiting injuries, explained about the fight out behind the barn. In turn, Ben and Jim related how they had finally located the free-graze wagon-camp by allowing their saddle animals to scent-out the remuda of free-graze animals, then they had stalked through the darkness until they saw the girl with a beltgun around her middle and one of those Springfield rifles leaning conveniently close, while she sat by lantern-light reading a book.

They had split up, Jim to approach from beneath the wagon where he could grab the butt of that rifle and prevent the girl from reaching for it, while Ben came round from behind the girl and attempted to pin her arms to her sides before she could draw the sixgun. It had been a hazardous enterprise and there had been several bad moments. Once, when some horses picked up the scent of the Wayland-horses and nickered, the girl had put aside her book to step away from the lamplight with a hand on her Colt, looking out into the night and listening. Another time when Jim stepped into the middle of some invisible black harness which had been indifferently dumped in the grass, Jim had unavoidably made a small sound. He recalled freezing in place, fully exposed and expecting the bullet which did not come. The girl had not heard him.

They both turned to look at her when they told the last of their tale, and Jim Vargas grinned from ear to ear. The moment Ben leapt ahead and pinioned her arms, she'd come up off the chair fighting like a cougar. She bit one of Ben's hands and kicked both his shins. She almost threw him backwards, but Jim had come forth from beneath the wagon to help, and she had finally ceased fighting.

Cliff and Johnny gazed admiringly at the big girl. She refused to look at them and sat there, red in the face, staring at the opposite wall.

George wanted to smile but he kept his face stonily impassive. The mental picture he had of that strong girl almost overwhelming two Indian bucks, and most certainly surprising them both with her power, was funny.

The girl turned slightly and watched his face closely, perhaps to see whether or not he was going to laugh at her, and when he looked stonily away she too turned her head.

Cliff arose to get some hot water from the stove and

take it over to the bunkhouse where he intended to wash out the bloody snarl in his hair, and to shave, both of them, things which should heighten his morale. Right at this moment he did not feel very good, victor or not. The last thing he said, before walking out into the dawn, was a question directed at Ben or Jim.

"How long will it take those bas—those other fellers—to get their recovered herd over to the wagon-camp?"

Ben had evidently already considered this. "Don't worry," he replied, "they'll be until maybe noon. If you're thinking about them reading the sign where we grabbed the girl, and returning over here loaded for fight, you can stop worrying. Jim blanketed out all the tracks."

Cliff went on out into the cold with his pan of hot water. Johnny, too, finally arose to depart. His arm was not as sore as it had been, but it was still there to remind him he had been injured every time he used it.

The remaining two riders ate and filled up on coffee, and finally Ben Chavez arose wiping his lips on a soiled sleeve. He caught the eye of Vargas and jerked his head. They walked out without a word or a glance at George or the captive girl. In the yard, they gathered up their horses and led them, including the girl's flashy chestnut gelding, to the barn. It was light enough in there for the chained men to recognize that horse at once.

Hiram Rockwell swore, then snarled savagely at the pair of dark-skinned Wayland-rangeriders. Ben and Jim eyed old Rockwell stoically and proceeded with the off-bridling, the off-saddling without an expression on their faces nor a comment on their lips. They knew the kind of men they were among.

"If she's hurt," said the old man, and did not finish it.

The lanky, youthful Rockwell called Andy, queried the riders in a civil tone of voice. "Mister Wayland told us where you fellers had gone. Mind telling us—is our sister all right?"

Ben turned, totally ignoring the old man. "She's all right," he said, and finished up with the chestnut gelding and led it out back to a corral. That was all either of them told the Rockwells. They finished their work, forked feed because it was that time of morning, then they both went wordlessly off to the bunkhouse. They were tired.

George was also tired and he presumed the handsome big girl was also, but except for refilling her coffee cup and relaxing at the table opposite her, he showed no interest in her probable tiredness and evinced no indication of his own bone-weary feeling.

He lit a cigarette and studied her smooth, tanned features, and said, "One of your brothers is favorable to paying me for the grass you people grazed off. I think the youngest one would agree with that too, but he hasn't said so. Listen to me, Samantha; what you folks did was worse than stealing my horses or rustling my beef. There's a drought; has been one for two years now. In order to stay alive every cowman in this territory has to manage his grass as best he can. It might be a little different if the grass had been rained on, but it hasn't. You've just about ruined this ranch."

"Fence us out," she snapped. "If you don't want cattle

on your land, fence them out, Mister Wayland. That's the law."

He said, "Not up here it isn't. But even if it was, what kind of people deliberately graze over another man knowing they'll probably bankrupt him?"

"All we knew was that there were no cattle when we came grazing through."

George's temper rose a notch. "You knew. Your paw and your brothers knew. We'd only moved the cattle to the foothills to save the home-place grass when you people arrived. You saw the sign because it was all around you."

"There were no cattle!"

He stopped speaking. If she had been one of her brothers he would have gone across the top of the table after him. She was using all the specious arguments free-graze men always used, not because she expected him to believe them, or concede, but because she was defiant and hostile. Ordinarily, his response to a *man* like that would have been a fight.

He sat looking steadily at her for a while, then he picked up his coffee and drained the cup. As he arose from the table he said, "Four hundred dollars today, Samantha. Yesterday it was three hundred. Tomorrow it will be the cattle."

She raised sulphurous large eyes to his face but did not open her mouth. She seemed to want to denounce him further, but was being held back by some sixth-sense, some female intuition which warned her that one more show of defiance from her and he was going to react with hot anger.

He waited, and when she did not respond, he said, "You know damned well I've got the right. Unless you're as warped and unreasoning as your paw, you know darned well any man's got the right to defend his land and his grass."

She suddenly said, "We don't have four hundred dollars. We might have three hundred, but there won't be four hundred. What do you think we are, idiots? If we had four hundred dollars why would we graze off other people's grass? We could lease good grassland, not the kind you had, and hold our herd in one place."

He studied her for a long moment, then returned to the table with the coffeepot. "More?" he asked, holding the pot poised.

She did not answer aloud but she pushed her cup forward. He filled it and set the pot aside, then resumed his seat opposite her. "What do you think you would do if you were in my boots?"

She answered forthrightly. "Probably the same thing you're doing. But I'm not in your boots."

"Where in hell will you people end up?" he asked her. "I've been hearing about the end of the trail for some darned free-graze trespasser for ten years; you won't be any different. Either your paw and your brothers will end up getting killed by some mad cowmen somewhere, or they'll end up killing some mad rangemen, and get hanged. Samantha, I've never yet heard a good word said about free-grazers, and everyone can't be wrong, can they?"

"Who appointed you our judge?" she demanded with spirit. "You have a big ranch. How did you get it?

Inherited it? We weren't that lucky, so you want to wipe us out."

"Oh hell," he said in disgust, "you are as useless to talk to as your paw. The pair of you are warped out of your minds. He's a damned lousy failure, and that's all he is. Blaming it on everyone else, or on every*thing* else won't change anything, Samantha. If you and your brothers keep going with him, always heading somewhere because you've heard there was good grass you could steal, I don't know how *you'll* end up, but I sure as the devil know how *they* will end up. Dead!"

She did not say a word. She reached to lift her cup and while she sipped black coffee from it she kept her large, gunmetal-blue eyes on him, then she put the cup aside and said, "You were bluffing. You're not going to try to lynch them."

"I'm not?"

She gently shook her head at him. "No. You're not the lynching kind, Mister Wayland. You're not even the gunfighting kind."

He did not dispute her, he simply said, "How many do you suppose you'll run across who won't try to kill them, Samantha? Somewhere, and I don't think he's too far off, there is a man waiting and willing. Believe it, he's out there right now . . . Me? I'm going to make your paw bleed a little, either by taking his cash or his cattle. I'd a darned sight rather have the cash, but either way I'm going to stump-break him from ever tres-passing on Wayland-grass again."

She said, "Take the cattle, Mister Wayland," and arose. "May I see them now?"

87

He had not intended for them to see her or for her to see them, but now he wavered, then Ben poked his head in the door and said, "Jim saw a rider far out a little while ago, George. My guess is that the other ones are tryin' to scout up the ranch. By now they sure as hell know the Rockwells aren't going to come back, and I sort of think they've probably figured out we got the girl too. You want to go over into the loft where Jim is, and see for yourself? I'll watch *her* until you get back."

George went to the door, held it for Ben to enter the warm cookshack, then winked at his rangeboss as he said, "Don't get too close to her, Ben."

The rangeboss showed big white teeth in a grin of his own. "I won't, don't worry."

11

GUNS!

Samantha Rockwell declined the offer of coffee from Ben Chavez but she spoke to him, and that was something she had not done before despite their nearly night-long acquaintanceship. She said, "What is he like to work for?"

Ben, in the process of filling a cup, glanced around. "George Wayland?" Ben turned back to finish filling his cup before replying. "He's fair and honest and everyone's the same to him." Ben went to the table, to the seat opposite her George had recently vacated to cross to the barn. As he sat and leaned to get comfortable Chavez eyed the big handsome girl. "But if you're askin' because you figure you can talk him out of anything, forget it. Once his mind is made up, he don't change it, and right now he's up against the wall without winter grass." Ben tasted the coffee, found it as bitter as tanbark straight off an oak tree, and did not mind.

The girl said, "I'm sorry for what happened to him," and Ben Chavez who was descended from generations of total realists, answered her roughly.

"He's got a barn full of sorries, lady. Right now what he needs is cattle feed."

She reddened. "The grass is gone and that's that. What's the sense of harping on it all the time?"

Ben cupped both hands around the cup and gazed down into it, momentarily, then he eased half around and rummaged for his tobacco and papers. He deliberately avoided looking at her.

He and Jim Vargas too had that knack; if something appeared futile to either of them—such as this conversation—they would simply ignore the speaker, would turn their attention elsewhere in the most infuriating and exasperating manner.

But when they were as intently concerned about something as Vargas now was while he and his employer squatted in the barn-loft opening, all their interest was concentrated upon it. Vargas described his first sighting of that far-away horseman, pointed to the place where the stranger had been, then made a sweeping arm-gesture to take in more range as he said, "The daylight'll make 'em *coyote,* but they got all that country to hide in, daylight or dark. It's open;

89

we dasn't ride out there."

George was not perturbed. "No need to ride out, Jim. Whatever they want is most likely right here."

George was wrong but it did not occur to any of them for several hours, and by that time Cliff and Johnny, looking worse but feeling better, were back abroad, and Johnny had even wrestled up a creditable meal, under the supervision of the big girl, something Johnny did not seem to object to at all. In fact he gave the impression that he liked it, which made Cliff look disgusted.

Ben and Jim Vargas went to the bunkhouse after eating to rest. Cliff and his employer took two big platters of fried meat and hoe-cakes to the barn for the Rockwells, then while Cliff went back for the coffeepot, Hiram Rockwell said, "Mister Wayland, you win. I'll give you the three hunnert dollars." He said this with no trace of customary fierceness in his tone or expression, and George was of the opinion that his sullen, uncomfortable sons had turned solidly against him in order for the older man to have made such a concession.

George rolled a smoke and lit it before saying, "Three hundred—that was yesterday, Mister Rockwell. Today it's four hundred and tomorrow it'll be—"

"Damn you," exploded the old man, pulling straight up where he sat. "I'll see you in hell!"

Andy, the youngest son turned savagely on his father. "You'll pay! We all agreed you would pay!"

"Three hundred," snarled the older man.

"*Four* hundred," snapped the tall youth.

"By gawd, boy, I don't have no four hunnert dollars!"

90

Andy did not relent. The other sons sat also glaring, but they were silent when Andy said, "Then you'll make it up in cattle."

"Are you crazy?" exclaimed the old man, turning fully towards his youngest. "What'll we have to sell when next we trail 'em down to rails-end? How in hell will we ever get paid off, if we commence givin' away cattle?"

One of the older sons snorted. "Paid! When have any of us got paid?"

"Just as soon as we can trail this herd to—"

"I've heard that so many times over the past three, four years, stated the elder son bitterly, "it don't even sound hopeful any more . . . I'm with Andy; give him cattle to make up the difference so's we can get out of these damned chains and really head for rails-end. I'm finished. I've had enough."

The old man railed at them. "A little trouble, a little adversity with a damned grasslander winnin' a few hands and the lot of you want to quit. You never got that from my side of the family, by gawd. . . . Sons! Hell's bells, I got more guts in m'girl than I got in all my sons!"

Andy turned as the old man opened his mouth to go on speaking. Andy looked at George and said, "He's got three hundred. We'll give you that and as soon as we're free we'll fetch in another hundred dollars worth of cattle."

"You go near that herd," yelled the furious old man, facing solid rebellion within his tribe for the first time, "and I'll shoot you down like wolves. You turn on your own flesh and blood—"

"*Be quiet!*" They all turned, even George. She was over there in the front barn opening with Johnny Welton, standing very erect, her gunmetal-eyes fixed upon her father. "What did you say—you'd shoot your own children?"

"Sandy, you didn't hear what they done to me!" roared the old man, facing back around.

"I don't have to hear," she hurled at him. "What kind of parent even *thinks* like that, let alone says it aloud against his own children?"

To George this was a startling revelation. The old man had raged at his sons exactly as he might have raged at total strangers who were opposing him, but when his daughter appeared and took the side of those against the old man, he seemed to want to justify everything, seemed unable to use the same anger against her. She must have argued with him before, because she stood her ground without giving an inch, and every time he opened his mouth she let him have both barrels—and he took it.

To George, who had never been married, did not remember his mother very well, had never had a sister and actually knew practically nothing about women, other than that some men were related to them, this drama between a father and daughter was enlightening. He had seen angry women before, of course, in town and upon rare occasions among the cow outfits, but they had never been angry at him, and he had never felt in any way involved. Now, he *did* feel involved.

Samantha Rockwell waited for her father to speak out

and say more, but he did not look to George as though he were going to speak at all. He looked from his daughter to the yonder morning-lighted yard and raised a chained hand to scratch his grimy beard stubble.

It was Cliff Howlett with his rough lack of tact who spoke next. He looked harshly amused as he said, "Old man, you got your match after all."

Rockwell whirled. He had reason to dislike Cliff and when George was certain one of those grisly promises of execution was about to be shouted into the hush, Samantha said, "Paw; I've told you before—you have been creating a rattlesnake-den. You've bullied your own children until you've turned them against you. And those three renegades you took into our camp . . . *Paw . . . !*"

Without a warning the flat, distant sound of a gunshot reverberated through the daylight and Samantha collapsed, striking Johnny, whose pure astonishment was so great he did not even fling out his arms to prevent her from falling until it was too late. She slid down his left side, and rolled flat out.

Men cried out. George saw Andy the youngest, and even the old man, struggle to his feet, straining at his chains as Johnny leaned, picked Samantha up and ran into the barn with her cradled in his arms.

Ben Chavez called from down by the bunkhouse and Cliff Howlett ran out the rear of the barn, sixgun in hand.

In a moment, the Wayland ranch-yard resembled an aggravated beehive. Men ran for carbines, and afterwards they scattered among the buildings seeking movement far out where that bushwhacker was lying.

George called Jim Vargas down from the loft and demanded to know whether Jim had seen the assassin. Jim looked at the girl on the ground and shook his head, then he went out the back way to join Cliff.

Johnny and George knelt. George told the cowboy to fetch a saddleblanket and roll it for a pillow, then he unbuttoned the girl's jacket. The blood was high and spreading. Her father groaned his pronouncement, "Lung-shot by gawd. Oh Lord, who did You let shoot my little girl like this?"

Johnny returned and George changed his mind about needing the pillow. "Help me carry her to the main-house," he ordered, "then saddle a horse and head for town for the doctor, Johnny."

One of the Rockwells warned them against moving her and although he may have been right in his dire predictions, they lifted her anyway and started out of the barn and southward along the west side of the yard in the direction of the main-house.

Cliff came from behind the house, Winchester in hand. He looked at the blood, the slack body and grey lips and said, "Dead yet?"

George almost snarled at him.

"I saw the son of a bitch," Cliff said. "At least I saw a horseman dusting it wide open to the west. He was far beyond carbine range."

That remark made George look out across his range at the same time he reached a conclusion. That marksman had been far too distant to wound the girl unless he had used a rifle, instead of a saddlegun. It *had been one of those other free-grazers then!*

Right at the moment he did not reflect upon the improbability of a free-graze man wanting to shoot a Rockwell. Later, though, that thought occurred to him. As he continued along with Johnny and Cliff, taking the unconscious girl into the house, he thought of something different.

It was still in his mind when he growled for Johnny to go to the cookshack and draw off a basin of hot water and fetch along all the clean rags he could find. Then, with Cliff standing in the doorway of the bedroom, watching, George peeled back the torn, soggy shirt to expose the wound.

The bullethole was very small, in front where it had exited, and in back where the slug had initially struck her. Cliff said, "Twenty-five-thirty-five, George. It wasn't no bigger rifle or it'd have punched a bigger hole in her."

George said, "Go rig out four horses, Cliff. One for you and Ben and Jim and me. Go on."

Howlett turned on his heel and marched out of the house.

George went to his medicine-chest and got some disinfectant, which was all he knew to do to a wound like this, and when Johnny returned George washed the wound, made a clean, neat bandage, and as he was finishing, the girl opened her eyes and drowsily gazed upwards. George forced a smile.

"You're lucky, Samantha. The bullet went plumb through and it was a right small calibre."

She stared for a long time, looked briefly at Johnny,

then turned her attention back to George. "He shot me?"

George said, "Who?"

"Buster."

George and Johnny exchanged a brief look then George started to dry his hands on a clean towel. "Someone sure as hell shot you," he told her. "If it was Buster—whoever he is—we're going after him. Samantha; lie easy. Don't thresh around. We'll get the doctor for you after a bit."

As George turned to depart Johnny said something about riding to Cibola for the doctor and George shook his head at him.

"It's a clean wound. She'll survive it. Anyway, I've changed my mind about that, Johnny. You stay on the ranch. I need someone here I can trust. I'll cut loose that big one down in the barn, the one called Andy, and send him for the doctor. Make sure the rest of them stay chained, and if any strange riders come anywhere near the yard—you know what to do."

George turned, saw Samantha watching, and smiled down at her again, then he walked away heading for the yard.

12

RIDERS ON THE TRAIL

The moment George entered his barn they all yelled at him almost in unison and he snarled them back into silence, then reported that Samantha was conscious and that her wound did not look fatal to him, did not in fact even look very serious.

He then cut loose the youngest Rockwell and told him to saddle a horse and ride down to town for the doctor. With all the others listening he also said, "Don't try to release your paw or your brothers. I want your word on that."

The rawboned youth nodded his head. "You got my word."

Cliff turned as Jim and Ben came through the rear barn opening, each one carrying a rolled jacket to lash aft of the cantle. It wasn't cold, and in fact as hot as it was out on the range it did not seem that it would ever again *be* cold, but the last few times Chavez and Vargas had ridden out, they hadn't been able to get back near a stove again before they had gotten cold. They were perfectly willing to go manhunting, but this time they were going fully prepared.

Cliff let the others finish with the rigging-out while he took Andy Rockwell out back to point out a good horse for the ride Andy had to make. While they were outside he also gave Andy some good advice.

"Don't cross George Wayland, and you'll come out of this all right. *Do* cross him, and you'll never stop wishing you hadn't."

Andy did not even act as though he had heard; he stepped through the stringers, snaked out a little bearcat loop and caught the horse he wanted. Cliff turned with a shrug and went back to the barn. Later, as the four of them were leaving the yard on horseback, he said, "George, I wouldn't put it past that young buck to set the other ones free, and if they do that, Johnny's in a lousy situation, with all them Rockwells running loose."

The only reply Cliff got was a curt one. "He won't do it. I trust him."

Ben and Jim heard that and impassively accepted it. What their *real* thoughts were no one would know. They rode quietly until, a couple of miles out, Ben gestured for Jim to cut wide, then Ben did the same but in the opposite direction. It had been out here, somewhere, that the assassin had been lying when he'd fired. Only one of them believed the bushwhacker hadn't been aiming at Johnny Welton, who had been standing beside the big girl, and his reason was based on something the big girl had said when she'd regained consciousness; she had been convinced someone named Buster had been shooting at *her.*

But for the time being George hardly more than passingly thought about this. It was not immediately important; what *was* that important was locating those other free-graze men.

George had another suspicion too, which was different from his speculations of a while back. He did not now believe those surviving free-graze men had ever intended to free the Rockwells.

He had no valid proof that this was a fact, but knowing something about the kind of men he thought those renegades might be, fairly well convinced him. Even so, he kept this to himself also, and when Jim Vargas gestured with an upraised arm which he swung in a little high circle, George turned aside calling for the others to ride with him. Jim's arm-signal had been the *wibluta* symbol to "come at once."

The tracks Vargas had discovered were fresh and had been made by one rider heading away at a fast gait. They turned to follow along, also at a lope, as the unknown rider had done, and Cliff signaled for Ben Chavez, who was watching from a considerable distance, to hurry along and catch up.

By the time Chavez caught up Jim Vargas had called for a halt. Here, in this latest place, were the tracks of two more horsemen. Cliff scratched his head. "Why in hell, if they all was together, didn't the other two ride on in with the bushwhacker?"

"Because," stated George, convinced finally of his theory, "they didn't any of them ever mean to cut the Rockwells loose, and these two which hung back probably only meant to keep watch and if they had to, protect the retreat of the assassin."

Cliff looked around. "If they didn't figure to get the others loose," said the cowboy, and slowly resettled his hat, then brightened. "I understand, George. . . . I *think* I understand."

Wayland grinned. "Then let's get to riding." He turned ahead and booted out his mount in another long-legged, loose lope.

Cliff caught up to him and while they were riding stirrup Cliff said, "They didn't figure to free the Rockwells because with the whole blessed family out of this, the herd and wagon and everything was theirs. Right?"

George nodded. "I think so. Something like that."

"Then," demanded the loping rider, "why in the hell

did they even bother coming over anywhere near the buildings? They'd have done a heap better to take those liberated cattle to join the balance of the herd, hitch up the wagon, and keep heading west."

This had been George's same original thought. Now, he thought quite differently and attempted to explain to his rider. "One of them, and I'd figure him to be the one with the most influence, had some reason for wanting to shoot the girl. . . . The others went part way and maybe agreed to cover his back, then he rode on up and waited until the chance came."

"But that feller was aiming at Johnny," stated Cliff, protestingly, because he believed this; all of them except George believed, and originally so had George. Now, the answer was different. "If he'd been aiming at Johnny," stated young Wayland, "he'd have hit him. He was aiming at the girl."

Cliff rubbed his bristly jaw and rode along for a while with nothing to say.

The tracks were abundantly clear even though there was that same peculiar perceptible haziness in the air which George had noted the previous night. It did not especially inhibit visibility but it prevented very much sun-glare from coming through. No one heeded it; it was in their favor in any case.

They were two-thirds of the way towards Blue Sump when they encountered some cattle wearing that lightning-strike Rockwell brand. The cattle only numbered perhaps twenty or thirty head and they did not flee at sight of loping horsemen the way range cattle invariably did.

Ben Chavez said, "Drop-outs; sore-feet or just too damned old to keep up."

He was correct. No one else commented but as they rode past the little band they looked them over. Mostly, they had to be gummers because their bones showed and they had scrawny necks, big bellies, and were rump-sprung.

A half mile farther Cliff said, "Hey, George; them's your share of the grazer's cattle."

Ben and Jim grinned at the look on their employer's face.

They hauled down to a walk when they detected the scent of a cooking-fire which had evidently been dying most of the day, but they did not see the wagon for another half mile and the reason was clear only when they changed course slightly in order to be following that smoke-scent. The free-graze camp had been made up-country from the vicinity of Blue Sump where there were some trees, and here someone had made a sturdier rope corral by weaving his ropes in and out among the trees.

George turned off the flat grassland heading for a distant arroyo, but Cliff said, "No point in it now. Look yonder."

He was right. There were two men leaning on those long-barreled rifles near the shady tailgate of the old camp-wagon, watching. They had clearly seen the Wayland-riders long ago.

Ben paused, dropped his reins and looked all around. He and Jim Vargas felt uneasy about that third renegade. *One* of them had demonstrated how efficient he was as assassin. If he was the missing one. . . .

"Out of range," said George, in response to the anxious looks of his riders.

Ben disagreed. "Maybe. But if that third son of a bitch is lying around out here somewhere with one of them rifles that shoots today and kills tomorrow. . . ."

George did not argue, all he said was, "I'll ride over there, part way, and palaver."

"You do that," exclaimed Ben, "and those two fellers with the long-barreled rifles can take you hostage like you done old Rockwell, and there won't be a damned thing Cliff and Jim and me can do about it. We got carbines. We couldn't even get close enough to support you, with carbines against them rifles."

"A better notion," put in Cliff, "would be to sashay around until we find the cattle, then turn them back towards the home-place. That'll pull those three devils away from their wagon into some place where maybe we can get a crack at them, rifles or no rifles."

Ben groaned. "All them cattle? Cliff; they'll finish off what grass is left, damn it all."

The decision was up to George. "They can't pull out unless we permit it," he explained to his riders, "and about now I'd say they want to pull out right bad. Before we free the Rockwells. The way *they* see it, it's got to be a Mexican stand-off, and now that they see us over here, they'll sweat a few more bullets."

"Let 'em sweat," growled Cliff Howlett. "What we'd ought to do is just set out here beyond rifle-range and stare 'em into the shivers—while one of us heads for Cibola in a hurry and fetches back the law and a posse."

Jim Vargas stepped down from the saddle without a word and sank to his knees, ears to the ground. The others watched and waited. When Jim arose to dust himself off he looked a little rueful. "Nothing," he reported.

Ben made a suggestion. "Jim can scout up the herd. It's got to be north of us, and maybe northwesterly if they pushed it last night, but anyway, it can't be too darned far. . . . We could stampede it to hell and back. That would tie those fellers down for a week, trying to find all their critters and get them bunched again."

George nodded towards Vargas. "Your scout," he said, and Jim grinned as he reined around to ride northward until he located fresh herd-sign. A man did not have to be a very exemplary tracker to find a big herd of cattle by their tracks.

George dismounted and stood at his horse's head. Cliff and Ben did the same. The three of them returned the steady stare of those two distant riflemen. George finally rolled and lit a smoke while Cliff reached for his cut-plug, then burst out swearing: old Rockwell had not returned the plug.

Ben laughed but Cliff did not think it was very funny that Hiram Rockwell, the raffish old devil, had deliberately neglected to return Cliff's plug of tobacco and his clasp-knife.

"Old bastard," exclaimed Cliff, accepting the makings from George, and going to work rolling a smoke. "That darned old underhand, crooked, snaky buzzard done that on purpose. They can't resist being dishonest; it goes with the breed of 'em."

Cliff lit up and squinted in the direction of those two watching men. One of them turned towards the rope corral as Cliff watched, and the Wayland-cowboy offered his opinion of this.

"He's going after Jim sure as hell. If we stay here and don't try to help Jim nor warn him, that louse over there just might sneak up on him."

George said, "I don't think he'll be too successful at sneaking up on Jim. . . . But those damned rifles make a big difference. When he rides out, Ben, track him—and be damned careful."

Chavez dropped his smoke and stamped on it. He would be careful. He would also be as sly as a wolf and as devious as a coyote.

Cliff said, "One left. We sure as hell busted them up, whether we figured to or not. Man for man I think we can clean them out."

That may have been true, all the same George had worlds of respect for those long-barreled rifles. As long as their adversaries had those weapons and knew how to use them, there was no safe way under the sun for George or his riders to get close enough to their enemies to risk a gunfight.

They stood in silence until the free-graze man passed in and out among the yonder trees and emerged in the open on Jim Vargas's trail. Then Ben Chavez swung up, turned away from his friends and walked his horse in a very large half-circle which would take him around the wagon-camp—out of range of the remaining man there—and would eventually put him on the trail of that distant stranger.

13

THE WAGON-CAMP

Cliff was eyeing the remaining rifleman when he said, "George, we can yank the slack out of this one. You commence going westerly while I ride easterly, then, when he can't be sure which one of us might get in close to him, we can peel some hide off him with the Winchesters from hiding." Cliff pointed up where their arroyo meandered rather aimlessly northwesterly, then he turned and squinted in the opposite direction. There were a few scanty trees in this other direction. Cliff raised an eyebrow and George nodded. Whether he was very confident or not almost anything was better than just standing there until Ben and Jim got back.

They rode off in opposite directions and the leaning man over at the distant wagon-camp took his rifle with him to a low tree-limb, swung down the *olla* for a long drink, replaced the pottery water-jug and twisted a little to his left to watch George departing. Not until the man had turned to also watch Cliff did it apparently dawn on him that they now had him between them, and rifle or no rifle, he was outnumbered.

He did not react with perceptible misgivings. He even rolled a smoke and lit it, with his long-barreled gun leaning against the same tree from which the *olla* hung suspended. Maybe he was outnumbered but he still had an equalizer which made the odds acceptable. As he smoked in tree-shade and looked from side to side, watching the pair of horsemen, George and Cliff got far enough away on each side of the little bosque of trees where the wagon-camp stood, to finally gradually alter course and start a long, walking-gaited ride on up and around the bosque of trees, and this maneuver pulled the watching free-graze renegade away from the *olla* tree in order to keep an eye on the riders.

He had to walk past the wagon, which cut him off from his sighting of George, and later, passing back and forth among the trees, he lost track of Cliff altogether. This made him anxious. There were arroyos out there, he knew for a fact, but the idea of losing one of those obvious enemies down into one such arroyo even though it had to be a great distance from his wagon-camp, was disconcerting.

He hurried on up past the wagon, past the rope-corral, out to the very edge of the last tree and leaned on his rifle scanning the eastward range yard by yard for some sight of Cliff.

It was as though the earth had swallowed Howlett up. None of those arroyos were actually long enough or deep enough their full length for a rider to pass down into them, and continue on his way riding through them out of sight for any very considerable distance.

George, slouching along upon the crooked edge of his more northwesterly gulch, was just as intrigued by the disappearance of Cliff Howlett as the distant rifleman was, with the exception that George knew his rangerider; whatever Cliff was up to, he would be serious about it, and right now he was certainly up to something. George also knew those criss-crossing ancient erosion gullies called arroyos. He knew them much better than the free-graze men knew them; George had been riding this same range all his life, and there was no way for Cliff to have disappeared down into one of those gullies—unless he had deliberately engineered that kind of a disappearance, and George knew how that could have been done.

He smoked, sat motionless upon the rim of his arroyo, and after a long wait during which he watched that intrigued and perhaps upset and wondering rifleman wander out of the trees a few yards, peering intently out where Cliff had sunk from sight, George decided on the course of action he must also follow. He laughed to himself about it.

The northwesterly arroyo was roughly six feet deep with grassed-over, very gradually sloping, sides which terminated where some prehistoric downpour had created this entire network of wide, shallow gullies.

Occasionally, over the centuries, there had been a storm of sufficient intensity to again send rivers of water boiling down through those run-off gulches, but it had not happened very often, otherwise there would not be grass and underbrush, and even an occasional tree, growing up from the bottom of the arroyos.

George rode into his gulch, dismounted, saw that all his horse had to do was raise his head to be partially exposed, and he walked back and forth until he found a broad, grassy place, and there he up-ended his horse with a blacksmith's throwing-hitch and left the indignant animal lying down there on the grass tied by all four ankles. As long as the horse was not left there too long he would manage very well. He would not like it for one moment; there was only one thing horses feared more than being left tied upon the ground, and that was the scent of a mountain lion.

George took his Winchester, crept to the edge of his arroyo and saw the distant rifleman beginning to back up, beginning to yield ground as though he were suddenly afraid. He retreated all the way back to the trees and for as long as George lay watching, the man did not re-appear. He was evidently keeping his vigil, now, from well within the protection of the trees. Finally, he was no longer casual nor self-assured.

George smiled to himself, slid back down to the arroyo's bottom, walked back where his indignant horse had decided to make the best of a very humiliating and unnerving situation by closing his eyes and relaxing as best he could, smiled, stepped past and under the horse's narrowed look of reproach, trotted back down the arroyo in a crouched position.

He hoped to be able to reach that bend in the arroyo which was only a hundred yards or so from the bosque of trees where the camp was. That was the only place from which he might even dare make a rush into the wagon-camp, and even that was not a very good place to take a chance—but—it *was* a good-enough place for a Winchester to duel with a Springfield rifle.

Beyond the arroyo there was neither sound nor movement, but that unique high haziness seemed to be strengthening. George leaned, twice, upon the uphill slope facing easterly when the sidehill was not very high, and peered out. He could see no one, neither the man with the rifle at the wagon-camp nor Cliff Howlett. He really had not been hopeful of seeing Cliff but he had rather hoped he might get some idea where the other man was. Apparently the stranger with his blasted rifle was taking no chances; he was somewhere back in the vicinity of the wagon, no doubt, perhaps belly-down with his Springfield cocked and ready to be swung in any direction.

For a moment, the last time he looked out, George spared a thought to the people back at the ranch. Mainly, he thought of the handsome big girl and her injury. He also reflected upon something which had been mentioned to him prior to his departure from the yard Johnny Welton was not in the best of all positions if those Rockwells got loose.

Then a high call floating down-land from the north somewhere scattered his other thoughts as George turned to look backwards.

He saw nothing. Moving along the near-bank to lean for a better look he still saw nothing. But obviously there was someone out there, so he stopped stock-still, blocked in spaces and examined each one minutely— and did not see anything moving or standing upright, or even mounted upon a horse.

He worried a little as he moved along, steadily approaching that place where his Winchester could reach over into the wagon-camp. The man whose shout he had heard just very well might be one of those other free-grazers on his way back to the wagon-camp.

The reason he ultimately abandoned this notion was because, by the time he finally got down where to that dog-leg in the arroyo which meandered very close to the bosque of trees, no one had appeared riding in the direction of the free-graze camp.

If that shouting man had been either Ben or Jim, then there was nothing to worry about. He slowed his approach for the last thirty or forty yards and came to the place where he only had to raise up slightly to be able to see the color of the paint on the running-gear beneath the old free-graze wagon, and halted for a final look rearward.

The land was still as empty up there as it had always been.

He shook his head, edged over along the eastward bank of his arroyo, leaned close and began to very gradually come erect. The bank was no higher than his shoulders at this particular place, evidently having been worn away by rainwater coming down from the bosque of trees into the gulch.

There were several horses in the rope corral, drowsing, swishing their tails, standing hipshot with their lower lips drooping and their eyes nearly closed. Someone had propped the wagon-tongue and had two sets of old chain-harness draped from it as though he had expected to harness the team and roll at any moment.

The tailgate had been chained up, which was an even better indication that someone had been on the verge of striking camp when the Wayland-riders had appeared.

George raised his carbine to settle it in the dirt and very cautiously ease it forward, but there was no target. If he had been rash by nature he might have been encouraged to crawl out of the gulch and make a dash for the shelter of the wagon, then take his chances from there. He wasn't that rash and never had been, but he *did* prise loose a round stone and pitch it overhand so that it dropped against the slack, soiled old canvas across the wagon's bows, and make a distinctly audible sound as it fell along the wagon-side and struck the ground.

Nothing happened. No one moved to give his location away, nor fired to show how nervous he was.

George ducked down to remove his hat, mop sweat, replace the hat and come back up again with a larger round stone in his hand. This time he pitched the stone as far as he could and it landed inside the rope corral. The horses swung to look a trifle skeptically, then, when there was nothing further to upset their naps, they resumed their earlier stances of complete indifference.

George leaned along the bank and made an intense study of as much of the camp as he could see, and did not find a place where he felt sure a man might be hiding. It worried him. He expected Cliff to be arriving upon the opposite side of the camp shortly now, and if that rifleman was this good at concealing himself, then he was probably just as good as an ambusher. For a fact, at least one of these men was an accomplished bush-whacker, and from what Hiram Rockwell had said, all three of these renegades were experienced and treacherous.

Then Cliff's unmistakable voice came down across the stillness in an almost conversational tone, and the words were almost friendly.

"Hey, gunsel, listen to me: I got a Winchester aimed square at your brisket where you're lyin' snug against that tree, and you can tell from my voice I'm darned well within range. Now just leave the damned rifle on the ground and stand up slow. Otherwise, gunsel I'm going to kill you."

George held his breath. For a long time there was not another sound after Cliff had spoken. George only knew Cliff was upon the opposite side of the bosque of trees, but how he had managed to get there was a mystery. He hoped very fervently that Cliff was not bluffing.

Cliff wasn't. He never bluffed, not even in poker.

The next time he spoke his voice was a little less amiable. "Mister; I'm not joking with you. Leave the gun lyin' and stand up. You got ten seconds then I'm going to put one right through you from front to back. *Stand up!*"

George caught movement and swung his saddlegun. A man slowly arose from a sickly stand of choke-cherries near the base of a large old tree. He did not have his rifle in his hands.

Cliff sounded friendly again when he said, "That's right obligin' of you, partner. Now you just stand there like you was carved out of wood."

George left his arroyo by stealth and came down through the trees in the direction of that standing, unarmed man. He saw Cliff stand up, finally, and he had several trees between himself and the man he had just captured. If that was how Cliff had managed to crawl this close, he had to be crazy. Just because the bracketed man at the free-graze camp had been unable to watch the nearer easterly range because of intervening big old trees was no guarantee that he would not decide to suddenly move ahead and around through those trees, and if he had done that he would certainly have sighted Cliff crawling closer.

George was already full of disapproval when Cliff saw him out through the rearward trees and welcomed his appearance with a sardonic call.

"Hey, cowman, we got us a gunsel!"

14

TOWARDS THE SHOWDOWN

Their captive was a lean, sinewy, slightly stooped man, about six feet tall but he did not look heavy enough to even cast a decent shadow, and he had a fox-like, narrow, thin face, tanned to the color of old saddle-leather.

George and Cliff looked at him and shook their heads. He was not a man either of them would have either team-roped with or even hired-on to work in the riding season. He looked mean and treacherous and shifty.

Cliff retrieved the man's rifle and looked at it, then swung it one-handed with great force and broke the breech. He dropped it and flexed his fingers, which tingled from the blow.

The stranger said, "Listen, fellers, I warn't the one as shot Sandy. That was Buster."

George accepted that. "Where is Buster?" he asked,

and the stooped, shifty-eyed man raised a long, thin arm to point. "Northward with the cattle; we was fixin' to pull out. Me'n Hubbard come back to pitch everythin' in the wagon and put the team on the tongue, then head out and come in behind Buster when he had the herd moving." The man knew who George Wayland was, because he said, "Mister, we was going to do you right fair; we figured to cut back seventy, maybe seventy-five head to make up to you for the grass."

George leaned on a big tree. "That was right decent of you," he said, "considering they aren't your cattle." He pointed to a suspicious bulge. "Cliff . . ." The cowboy stepped up, yanked the free-graze man's shirt loose and lifted out a concealed Colt double-action Lightning .38. Cliff turned the little heavy weapon over and over, then shoved it into his own waistband, and returned to go over their prisoner again. This time he came up with a stiletto-type long bootknife which made Cliff's lip curl. He heaved the knife over his shoulder without even looking to see where it landed.

George asked the man his name and got a crooked smile which showed small, uneven, discolored teeth. "John Smith, if it's all right with you, Mister Wayland."

George ignored that. "When is Buster coming back?"

"He ain't. We was supposed to rig out the wagon and meet him on the trail, like I already told you."

Cliff studied their prisoner a moment, then slowly turned. George understood the look because he was thinking the same thing. He gestured with his Winchester. "John Smith, lead out the team, hitch them, and let's get rolling. What do you fellers do with your loose saddlestock?"

"Just sort of let 'em trail after, Mister Wayland. They been doin' it long enough, Lord knows." The prisoner smiled at George. "All I did was drive cattle. That's all. I never tried to make no trouble for you fellers and I even tried to tell Buster not—"

"Why did he try to kill the girl?" asked George, cutting across the shifty-eyed man's whining talk.

"Well," replied the prisoner, "that goes back a long ways, Mister Wayland, and as near as I know it was a personal thing."

"How personal?"

"Well, Mister Wayland, Buster's been fairly well sold on Samantha Rockwell since about the time us three fellers joined up."

"And she didn't reciprocate, so he shot her," said George.

"Something like that," agreed John Smith. "I told him, last night, we could likely make it clean out of the country if we'd just make a gather and get to moving. But no; seems they had a big argument few days back and Buster—well—Buster is a bad man to cross; he broods a lot."

Cliff looked at the corralled horses as he said, "Buster's a real nice feller, isn't he? Come on, string-bean, let's get the harness on that team."

George went over to look in the wagon while his rider and their captive snaked the harness horses from the rope corral. The wagon was full of the usual camp gear, plus a number of bedrolls, some old rusted branding irons, odds and ends, plus several Springfield rifles upon rawhide ties along the wagon-bows. Everything which had recently been loaded into the wagon had evidently been pitched in by careless and indifferent hands, but otherwise it was possible to see that someone—and he guessed about that—had at one time been very neat and orderly inside the wagon.

He moved forward when Cliff and the thin, stooped man led up a team of handsome big sixteen or seventeen hundred pound draft animals to be harnessed. He walked on past, out as far as the northernmost trees of the little bosque, and scanned the entire countryside. That man who had called out a half hour back was still out there and George was still curious about him.

Eventually, when he went back, Cliff was ordering the free-graze man to yank down his rope corral and free the saddle-stock. George noticed that Cliff never once allowed "John Smith" to get near him.

While they stood watching the renegade take down his corral, Cliff said, "That worthless, wore-out bastard would back-shoot his own mother. What'll we do with him?"

George answered while still watching the captive at work. "We'll trail up and find Buster and the herd, and we'll let John Smith sit on the wagon seat when we get up there so Buster will think everything is as it's supposed to be—then we'll nail Buster. I'd guess by then Jim and Ben had ought to have nailed the other one." George watched the freed horses head for grass and said, "I've got to go turn loose my saddle animal. Where is yours?"

116

Cliff pointed. "Yonder a mile or less, hog-tied down in the ditch. I'll get him as soon as we're—"

"You stay with John Smith and the wagon," said George. "I'll turn both of them loose and fetch back our saddles, and we can hide them inside the wagon. I don't think we'll have much trouble slipping up on Buster."

George left them and returned to his arroyo, went all the way back where his horse lay, freed the animal, then rode him overland in the direction of the arroyo where Cliff Howlett had left his horse.

This time, George had more trouble. Cliff's horse was a colt who was not philosophical about things because he was just simply too young. He didn't evince much sense either; all the time George was trying to free his ankles the colt was simultaneously trying to kick George.

Eventually, though, the colt was freed, got to his feet, was allowed to stand a few moments while George yanked loose the saddle, removed the bridle, then turned both the animals loose.

His intention, whether he caught the remaining two free-graze men or not, was to ride back to the ranch with the wagon. For that he and Cliff did not need their saddle animals. Also, George did not want any horses bearing his tomahawk brand with the wagon when they eventually reached Buster. He did not want to do anything to make the leader of the remaining free-graze men suspicious. He already knew enough about Buster—he was a quick man with a weapon, and he was also an accurate one.

Cliff tooled the wagon over where he could see

George, and when he got over there he curtly ordered "John Smith" to alight and help George pitch their riding equipment into the wagon.

"John Smith" was tractable. He was so friendly and co-operative and congenial that Cliff's dislike turned to solid distrust. He did not like the idea of their captive sitting upon the wagon-seat with them, but he had no intention of allowing "John Smith" to climb in back where those rifles still hung from wagon-bows, either, so he suffered the crafty-faced man to sit between them, and that way at least if "John Smith" got clever, if Cliff didn't settle his hash George would.

But the prisoner did not show the least bit of slyness nor antagonism. Each question George asked him, he seemed to answer forthrightly; even when George finally asked him if he and his two friends were wanted by the law, his answer was: "Yes sir, Mister Wayland. Me'n Hubard Wray is wanted in Wyoming. Hud's wanted bad; me, all I done was stop a couple of stages."

"Not as John Smith," stated Cliff dryly.

"No sir, not as John Smith, gents, but under m'true name of Earl Spencer."

"Where is Buster wanted?" George asked.

"Wyoming, Colorado, and I believe in Texas," was the reply. "I know he's wanted for stoppin' coaches and also for murder, 'cause he told us that one night when we was having a few drinks in a town south of here a few hunnert miles. He's been a hired gunman, too. He done told us that."

Cliff said, "What's his last name?" and got an immediate reply.

"Munser. Buster Munser."

"John Smith"—Earl Spencer looked amiably at first one of his captors then at the other one. "Gents, I been co-operating and I ain't through yet at lendin' you a hand," he said, then gazed expectantly at George Wayland. He did not seem to be very hopeful, where Cliff Howlett was concerned, and if this were so, then it indicated that the renegade was a good judge of men; Cliff would not have even answered a plea for mercy.

As it turned out, George was not very co-operative either as he returned the outlaw's gaze, and without comment negatively shook his head.

They drove up-country across an endless parched landscape where the tiny, frail shoots of grass were wilting and where dust came to life under their wheels as though they were crossing a desert. The only blessing was that lingering, long mistiness which seemed to be steadily but not very rapidly increasing as this long day wore along.

George and Cliff looked for Ben and Jim without being rewarded by any movement at all, on either side or far ahead. George worried but he did not allow the others to know it. Then their rat-featured and crafty-eyed prisoner pointed northwesterly.

"Dust. Faint, and it's a long ways off, but it's out there." He dropped his arm to a bony knee and continued to narrowly squint in the direction of that faint heavenward discoloration. "Buster's worth three men at movin' cattle, gents." The renegade looked at Cliff, then over at George. "Where's your two friends?"

Neither George nor Cliff knew, nor did it help any to

be asked such a question by a man who, despite his insistent congeniality, had to deep-down wish the worst for Jim and Ben, along with Cliff and George.

Cliff countered by saying, "Where's that feller who rode out of the trees?"

"Hub?" replied Earl Spencer. "He'll have seen them two fellers trailin' after him and he'll either have quit the country or he'll set up an ambush. I figure he'll use the ambush; after all, if us three can make it away with the cattle, we can sell out and be sort of rich, can't we?"

Cliff was not interested in the digression, only in Hubbard Wray's ability to bushwhack Chavez and Vargas. "If he nails them," Cliff snarled, "you're as good as dead."

Spencer's eyes widened. "Me? Why me? It's *him* that'll bushwhack 'em, not me. In fact I haven't done nothing much to no one, except maybe help the Rockwells fetch their free-graze cattle onto Mister Wayland's grass, and after all I'm only riding for Hiram and I got to do what I'm told to—"

"Oh shut up," growled Cliff in monumental disgust, and raised his free arm to point. "George; that's a horseman up ahead. See him; he's settin' still and watching us like maybe he's waiting for the wagon to come up."

George had seen the distant, motionless silhouette and he had also arrived at an unpleasant conclusion, which he now passed on. "If it's the one named Hubbard Wray, Cliff, then where in hell are Ben and Jim?"

"Ambushed," muttered Howlett, but George did not think so for a very good reason.

120

"I didn't hear any gunshots."

Cliff yanked down his hatbrim to try and make out that distant horseman better, but he could not do it so he reached down to loosen the Colt in his hip-holster and clucked up the team a little to close the gap faster.

They had covered a mile more or perhaps slightly less when George swung around on the seat and dropped down into the bed of the wagon. "Give Spencer the lines," he told Cliff. "That's not Jim and it's not Ben."

Cliff obeyed, their prisoner took the lines, and as he too strained ahead for an identification of the distant horsemen, he did not look too happy. He had an excellent reason not to feel too pleased; he had two armed and willing men behind his back and up ahead, whoever that was awaiting the wagon's arrival, he was not likely to be very congenial either, not even if it was Hubbard Wray and he thought Earl Spencer was alone on the wagon-seat.

For a while, as they drove along, the driver sat hunched like a big stork, saying nothing and concentrating upon the horseman, but finally he loosened a little in abject resignation and said, "Hell; that's Hub all right."

George and Cliff did not have much time to speculate on how Wray could be up there alone, when both the Indians had gone after him. The closer they got to the waiting rider, the more it became clear that Earl Spencer was correct, the man up ahead was not only the other outlaw, but he was also armed with a handgun and also with a saddlegun.

15

ENEMIES!

George touched the thin outlaw on the seat in front of him with the tip of his gunbarrel when he said, "Don't even try to wink at him."

Earl Spencer clucked at the team acting as though he had not been spoken to. When they came closer he called ahead. "Hey, Hub, there was two of them Wayland-riders took out behind you. You seen 'em?"

The thickly-made, swarthy man with the long-barreled rifle balanced across his lap answered shortly, "Yeah; I led 'em into some trees then lost 'em and headed back for you. I think they taken off to catch up with Buster . . . Stop that gawddamned wagon and listen to me!"

Earl Spencer hauled back, then dropped the lines.

The mounted man was nervous. He looked down-country in the direction from which the wagon had come. "Where's them other Wayland-riders?" he asked, leaning for a better look back. "Earl, saddle up one of the light animals, hand me out the old man's iron box, and let's us get the hell out of this. . . . Them two that was after me was redskins; one was 'Pache sure as I'm setting here."

Cliff stood up very slowly off his knees. So did George. The mounted man saw Cliff first, and did not see George until he had whirled his horse to fire the rifle.

Earl Spencer, tight-wound as a steel spring without seeming to be, suddenly leapt into the air and sailed off the wagon-seat with an outcry, flinging the lines from him.

That rifle exploded with a stunning sound, and Cliff flinched. George saw him do it as the mounted man kicked free and threw himself sidewards off his panicking mount. The big harness-horses also reacted to that terrifying explosion with a tremendous jump, and that spoiled the aim of both Cliff and George, but they might not have hit the outlaw anyway, because he was leaving the saddle, was falling to the ground between them and his horse, when they fired, but as the wagon careened when those team-animals lunged, Cliff was knocked backwards and rolled deep into the interior of the wagon cursing at the top of his voice.

George climbed to the seat, got down into the boot, clawed three times for the jerking lines before finally snagging them, then he climbed to the seat, braced both feet and hauled back at the same time trying to loudly talk the frightened big horses down from their runaway charge.

He managed it, but they had covered two-thirds of a mile before he got the animals to turn, to cut a swath out over the range which covered more than a half mile before they were heading back in the direction from which they had come.

There were two men on foot back there, both of them trying frantically to talk their way up to that skeptical horse from which the man named Hubbard Wray had thrown himself. The loose horse kept just beyond reach.

Cliff came clawing his way up front. He was without his hat and he had a bruise on his forehead where he had collided with some solid object during his free-fall inside the wagon. He had one of those Springfields in one hand and was clutching at anything handy as he painstakingly worked his way forward during the wild, tumultuous ride southward.

Finally, Earl Spencer decided neither he nor his friend were going to be able to catch that saddled loose horse. Spencer had the unhorsed man's Springfield. He threw himself belly-down and hauled the rifle around to aim in the direction of the oncoming wagon. There was not much danger of him hitting either of the men behind those huge team horses, but if one of those animals was downed in his harness, that would mark the end of George's and Cliff's pursuit of the free-graze man they wanted most of all: Buster Munser.

George jumped up onto the rocketing seat, aimed with his Colt over the ears of the big horses, and fired. Again, those huge beasts lunged. The only thing to prevent George from losing his footing and being catapulted backwards from momentum was Cliff—he shouted angrily and leaned as hard as he could to hold George upright with one hand, while clinging desperately to a wagon-bow with the other hand.

George fired twice more, none of his bullets hit Spencer, but each one must have disconcerted him because he had not fired the rifle when the running horses almost charged over the top of him. He let out a great scream, began frantically rolling, and left the Springfield rifle directly in the path of the wagon.

George could not talk the horses down to a walk this time, so he braced to use the lines, and Cliff Howlett bumped and bounced and clawed his way over into the seat also, then shoved all his weight on the wheel-brake. That made the difference. The blocks held, the large hind wheels locked, and the laden big wagon slowly wore down its powerful team.

George saw the pair of outlaws running. One of them, shorter and thicker than his companion, turned to fire his sixgun. It was a wild shot. George looped the lines, sprang out of the wagon and ran to retrieve that rifle Earl Spencer had dropped. It was useless; the breach was badly damaged from being run over by both a front and a rear steel tyre.

As George hurled the damaged rifle away and turned back towards the wagon for one of those guns hanging inside, Cliff jumped up onto the wagon-seat and began to frantically gesture. He did not fire at the fleeing men, he simply stood up there swinging his arms, and finally he also began to profanely shout. Slowly, George turned, then halted and watched.

Two riders were not even hurrying as they rode steadily to block off the flight of Spencer and Hubbard Wray. It was the rangeboss and Jim Vargas. Where they had come from, during the runaway and the hectic little battle, George had no idea but that was without a question who it was angling casually, almost indifferently, across in front of the afoot, hard-running free-graze renegades.

Cliff jumped out of the wagon and would have started legging it out there, behind the pair of fleeing men, if

George hadn't called sharply to him.

"Damn it, Cliff, mind those horses! If there is any more gunfire they're going to run again and we're going to get set on foot!"

Cliff turned back, reluctantly, then he and George watched as the pair of fleeing men suddenly looked around and saw a pair of armed horsemen diagonally cutting them off.

George was certain there was going to be another gunfight. There probably would have been except for one thing: Spencer and Wray, always before safely beyond Winchester range, now had nothing but one pistol between them.

When Ben and Jim were in position, Ben called for Jim to halt, and they both swung off on the far side of their animals, raised cocked Winchesters and gently laid them across saddle-seats. The best Colt sixgun ever made did not have the range of a saddlegun.

The pair of outlaws suddenly halted in their tracks. Wray, with his gun dangling from his right side, turned and said something to the taller, thinner, more stooped outlaw. Immediately, Earl Spencer called ahead.

"We wasn't figurin' on fightin' you boys. We was just tryin' to get away in case old Buster come along and seen us. He'll shoot us sure, because we want to go on back and he'p Mister Wayland."

Cliff heard that. So did George, who was breathing hard from the exertion. Cliff said, "Did you ever hear such a gawddamned forked-tongued son of a bitch before in your whole blasted life? George, I'm going to get me one of those rifles from inside the rig and kill that—"

"Cut it out," growled George. "Leave the rifles where they are. You knew what he was before this ever happened."

Farther out, Ben and Jim were mounting up again, were gesturing with their carbines for the pair of outlaws to turn and walk back in the direction of the wagon.

Cliff's hostility and disgust were too strong for him to control them for a long while. He and George stood beside the wagon watching the sweating, breathless, disarmed outlaws being herded back, and Cliff could not feel a single mote of pity.

"We should have killed that skinny, worthless devil," he muttered. "We'd ought to take time out right now to yank the horses off the tongue and prop it into the air and hang the pair of them."

George did not answer. He picked up the damaged Springfield, flung it over the tailgate and walked back up front where the big horses were now standing in drowsy contentment. He shook his head at them, then, without comment, started to manufacture a smoke as the pair of outlaws came up and halted near where Cliff was standing.

As George lighted up he strolled over there to ask his rangeboss a question. "Where did you two come from? We thought you'd gone on out to find the herd and the other one of these men."

Ben answered as though having two outlaws in front of him were the most normal thing in the world. "That's where we went, George, out and around this short feller here, and kept going until we saw the herd and that feller with it. Then we turned back to gather up the short feller—and hell—there you and Cliff was, running those big horses back and forth and yelling like Comanches, and these two looked to us like they was trying to get clear so's they wouldn't be run over." Ben grinned. He was teasing George and Cliff. George understood it, but Cliff was not in a receptive frame of mind. He scowled, and glared at Earl Spencer.

"Now tell us," he snarled, "you flung yourself down with that old rifle, because you was just too tired to stand up.

Spencer studied Howlett's face for a long time, then must have decided Cliff was not going to listen to another of his stories, and simply looked crestfallen without opening his mouth.

Jim Vargas dismounted and went up to Hubbard Wray, looked him squarely in the eye for a moment without saying a word, then Jim started a careful search and turned up a bootknife and a belly-gun. The latter was one of those little pepperbox models which had no accuracy unless the man holding it was less than a room's length from his prey, but it threw a lot of those little pellets, so eventually someone was bound to be injured.

As Cliff had done with the Colt Lightning he had taken from Spencer, Jim examined the unique belly-gun, then pocketed it and went on with his search. When he was finished he grinned at Hubbard Wray and went over to stand by his horse again.

George wondered whether the man they especially wanted might have been able to hear those gunshots or not. Cliff thought he must have, but Ben Chavez was doubtful. "There are a lot of bawling cattle, up there, and he's at least three miles distant. . . . But maybe."

George decided not to use the wagon in trapping Buster Munser after all. If he *had* heard gunshots, he would be far too wary now to be fooled by the wagon. Also, if he was suspicious and a fight ensued, no one in a laden wagon would be able to overtake a desperately fleeing man on a fast saddlehorse.

He said, "Cliff, you and Jim take the wagon and this carrion back to the ranch and wait for us. Ben and I'll find Buster Munser and fetch him along."

Cliff, for once, did not argue. "Bring him back tied across his saddle," he grumbled.

Vargas swung off and handed the reins of his animal to George, with a broad smile. That was about the only time when Jim's ugliness was alleviated, when he smiled. George winked, slapped the Navajo on the shoulder, and jutted his jaw in the direction of the demoralized prisoners.

"Don't let Cliff eat them alive," he said, and they laughed a little, then George stepped up across the saddle with the too-short stirrups, accepted the Winchester Vargas offered him, and jerked his head at the rangeboss. The last they saw of the prisoners and the wagon was from almost a mile out. The wagon had turned in a southeasterly direction and was steadily plodding along. It would not even get close to the ranch before dark, but that would not make much difference to the pair of Wayland-riders. They would have food in the back of the rig to eat, and they would have their prisoners to watch like hawks.

Ben led away in a swinging lope. He knew where the free-graze cattle had been a couple of hours earlier, and they could not possibly be more than another mile or two onward.

Once, Ben halted to study the misty heavens, and shake his head before turning his attention to George when he made a comment.

"I hope Cliff and Jim don't run into a yardful of those Rockwells when they get home."

George did not think this would happen. "I like the youngest one, Ben. The others I got doubts about, but the one they call Andy—I'll bet he's trustworthy."

Ben sighed, lifted his reinhand to head out in a lope again, and did not even look at George when he said, "I kind of thought you might like the girl too, George."

16

DEATH AND THE MIRACLE!

Even if they'd had no dust to go by, they could have located the herd. There were too many moving animals not to leave a powerful scent behind them, and not to be audible once George and Ben got well northward.

They had to alter their course a little because the cattle had done the same and were now heading in the same direction George and his riders had pushed their tomahawk herd. There was small danger of intermingling; the Wayland cattle were too many miles away over in the direction of the foothills.

Ben finally saw the moving mass and pointed it out to his employer, then they talked a little, planning strategy, and continued to ride forward side by side, believing it was possible for the man up there with the free-graze cattle to think George and Ben were his two partners Earl Spencer and Hubbard Wray.

There really was no need for an elaborate scheme; their mission was simply to find Buster Munser and collar him as the last of the free-graze trespassers. They had no illusions about how long they could fool him, even from this great distance. They also were aware that without the camp-wagon, they were not even likely to get very close to him before the battle began.

But they had one advantage, there were two of them and he was alone. What George worried about as they rode in the direction of the herd was whether Buster Munser had one of those Springfield rifles. If he had one, then they were only going to be able to get close enough to him to use their weapons of lesser range providing he made a mistake or got careless.

When they finally located him George had a fleeting thought that they were not going to get very close after all. He was sitting his horse in the middle distance watching their slow approach, and he unmistakably had one of those rifles balanced across his lap.

He was erect and clearly wary. Whether he had heard the earlier shooting or not, he was clearly suspicious as he sat out there backgrounded by the moving herd, eyeing the pair of slowly approaching horsemen.

The cattle had been kept moving by this one man, which was quite a feat even for a tophand. Normally, one man could control no more than a hundred head and unless he could manage to keep them bunched he could not control that many. The herd up ahead was many times larger, and this was normally their grazing time of day.

Whatever else the man up ahead was, he certainly was an experienced herdsman. Ben said something about this as they watched the herd begin to fan out, to destroy the control their herder had maintained up until now. Ben also professionally mentioned this.

"He won't have them for long now; look how the leaders are spreading out to graze. George, I think he's figured who we are and has decided to forget about the cattle."

It looked like a reasonable assumption. George continued to ride along and continued to study the motionless silhouette of man and horse far ahead.

The land was rougher up here, there were more broken places, more small arroyos without any of them being as deep as the gullies farther southward. There were no trees at all, for many miles. Riders in this territory were exposed; there was no way for them to employ natural means for concealment, and that, to George and Ben, gave Buster Munser's long-snouted old Springfield rifle an even greater importance. Normally, this time of year there would have been tall grass; tall enough to hide a prone man. Not this year and not the previous year.

George finally said, "Well, Ben, we've got to turn the

cattle anyway," and Ben began nodding his head as he poked along. That was true enough; sooner or later someone would have to take steps to prevent a collision, and an intermingling, of the two herds, Wayland's tomahawk-branded critters and Rockwell's lightning-branded critters. Not for several days, true, but eventually, and right now what George had in mind was the only means he could come up with to negate that Springfield rifle, short of attempting a bluff, and that idea had no appeal at all, not as long as Munser had that rifle.

"Bust 'em out right over the top of him, heading them east," Ben said. "He'll do his damndest to get above or below them."

George saw the distant figure shift the position of his Springfield, and had no more to say until Munser took up his fresh stance facing fully in their direction, the rifle held across the bend of one arm, Munser's hand at the breach within inches of the trigger-guard. He could throw the gun to his shoulder with one movement. Ben and George were not within range yet but they were close.

"He's not going to let us get very close," Chavez remarked.

"Then we'd better split up and head out and around to get behind the cattle," replied George. They said no more, but gradually widened the gap between them, and the watcher up ahead guessed their purpose, at least he guessed they were going to try and get him between them where he could not very hopefully fight them both simultaneously. Munser wasted a few minutes watching, but he finally began dropping back, which was one of his options; this was not only very large territory, but there were slackening-off, walking cattle back there Munser could try and put between himself and the men who were now obviously not his friends.

George watched too, and so did Ben Chavez, but their view was different. Maybe Munser could buy time by working his way in among the cattle, but there was an inherent peril to that course, too.

George glanced out where Ben was riding, then changed his own course to approach the cattle from his left, from southwesterly, and he saw Munser watching him so intently he only belatedly glanced around occasionally to see where Ben was.

Why the outlaw should be concentrating so hard on George was a minor mystery, and right at this moment George was not very interested in the reason, all he wanted to do was get southward of the herd, then begin turning as he rode, to get around behind at least most of the animals.

Munser finally seemed to guess what George and Ben were up to. He twisted to study Ben's position for a few moments then swung forward and urged his horse in George's direction, his intention clearly to reach rifle-range before George understood and moved farther away.

The trouble for Munser was that George, and also Ben, already were leery of his long-barreled weapon. The moment he turned in George's direction, George yielded ground and in the opposite direction Ben Chavez began feeling his way southward behind

Munser, weaving in and out among the cattle. So far, the herd had paid very little attention to a pair of strangers on horseback, and in a sense this was favorable; at least it allowed Ben and George to have some protection if they should suddenly need it.

Buster Munser kept trying to get close enough to get in at least one rifle-shot at George, and conversely George, with no intention of permitting that to happen, especially since he was aware how good a shot Munser was, kept moving farther away.

Finally, Munser halted, watched George working back through the herd towards the far side, then did something to his rifle, turned his horse and suddenly sank in the spurs.

The moment George saw Munser making a dash at him, George unshipped his Colt, ran at the nearest bunch of cattle and began firing into the air. The cattle whirled without any hesitation and broke away southeasterly in a stampede.

Ben, farther northward, also turned on the herd and began firing. Shortly, all the cattle were stampeding—and Buster Munser was half way through the herd, roughly in the centre of it and trying to penetrate deeper at a fast gait when the stampede began.

He whirled suddenly and, riding bent low, urged his horse toward one side of the herd, but the cattle were far too strung out, the result of their drifting away in different directions to graze an hour or so earlier. Munser could not make it.

He tried as hard as he could ride to rowel his mount through, but as the floodtide of stampeding cattle swept closer his horse continually bumped and was staggered by big hurtling bodies.

Munser dropped the rifle, drew his Colt and leaned to begin shooting the cattle that were threatening to upend him, and his horse. His gunfire only aggravated an already perilous situation. All three men were firing now, but along with gunshots Ben and George were also fanning the cattle and screaming at them.

Munser finally tried to turn straight easterly and run *with* the stampede. His horse actually gained for a time, and perhaps if it had been fresh, and if Munser had turned this way first, he might have been able to out-run the panicked cattle.

He went down, finally. Ben and George saw him disappear down into the churning mass of heaving hides. Then they saw the horse somehow manage to stagger upright and plunge onward for another dozen yards before it was knocked off its feet a second time.

That time, neither the horse nor its rider arose.

George hauled back to blow his horse, looped the reins to reload his shot-out sixgun, and when Ben rode up to halt nearby and do the same, George watched the dust begin to settle. The cattle still made the ground underfoot reverberate although they were now departing rapidly from this fatal area. Their dust, and their smell, would linger for another hour or two.

Ben holstered his weapon, waited patiently for George to do the same, then he jerked his head and they rode out there.

Munser and his mount had been run over by at least two-thirds of the free-graze herd. There was nothing anyone could do for either of them, and because neither George nor Ben had an extra horse to bring back the remains upon, they tarried only very briefly then wordlessly kept right on riding in the wake of the stampeding cattle.

There was nothing to say. Not for a long while at any rate. George rolled and lit a smoke and Ben simply rode along looking for the distant cattle. When he finally saw where some of the older animals had run out of breath and were now either standing head-hung panting, or were beginning to graze again, he said, "It's a hell of a way to die, but I think that man deserved it." Then Ben smiled at his boss. "Better him than one of us."

George could not disagree with that, so he smiled back and pointed up ahead where more of the winded cattle were stringing out left and right, going back to the business of grazing. It was while George had his pointing arm out that something cold struck the back of his hand. He pulled back and looked, then he very slowly raised his head.

That unique mistiness he had been observing without much actual interest the past couple of days, had become something a lot of cowmen had despaired of ever seeing again.

Rain clouds.

Only this time it was just one immense, low, dark blanket stretching the full width and depth of the sky from the eastern horizon to the westernmost rims and ridges, and it was looking increasingly ominous. In fact, Ben removed his hat to look at the layered dust and saw the miraculous little dark places, like stains, where raindrops had struck the bone-dry felt.

He put his hat back on and also rode along for about a hundred yards studying the sky. Finally he said. "By gawd, George—by gawd!"

They smelled the coming storm, felt the roiled remnants of a high wind blowing, and almost rode right on through the calmed-down free-graze cattle being unaware of their presence.

"Broke the back of the drought," exclaimed Ben Chavez. "This is going to break the back of the drought!"

The rainfall began to increase, slowly at first, and with small drops, then with larger drops and with a greater volume of them. Finally, when George and Ben finally stopped having any reservations at all, and tried to slump down making of themselves smaller targets, the water began coming down with a driving, stinging intensity, indicating that this particular downpour was not going to end for many hours.

George booted his horse over into a lope and held him to it until he had his distant log barn in sight, and by then he and Ben Chavez were soaked to the skin, and were not the least bit annoyed by this. It was the first time in two years, but most important of all, as they rode through the downpour, they could watch the earth and not see one single rivulet of run-off. That was how dry the range was.

17

A SUCCESSFUL FUTURE

There were at least a dozen men around the ranchyard when George and Ben made a bee-line for the rear entrance of the barn and swung down as they crossed the threshold, but most of them were either at the bunkhouse or upon the opposite side of the yard, at the cookshack. The men George saw when he stepped forth into the gusty lantern-light were the Rockwells, and they were no longer chained. Jud Porter, the town constable from Cibola was also in the barn, putting on a long yellow rider's slicker as Ben and George charged in.

A couple of townsmen jumped out of the way when the horsemen flung off inside the barn, and one man started to reach for his carbine, leaning upon the logs, when Ben Chavez looked disapprovingly and said, "What the hell do you think you're going to do?"

The townsman did not complete his grab and neither did he explain what he had had in mind. Constable Porter walked back, eyed the pair of dripping rangemen, then said, "George; we got them other two—Spencer and Wray—over at the cookshack. We also got old Hiram Rockwell over there . . . Where is the other one—the feller called Munser?"

"Dead," George replied. "Stampeded into jelly out on the northwesterly range, Jud, and I'd appreciate it if you'd have him hauled away as soon as possible."

"Why didn't you fetch him on in?" demanded the indignant lawman, "Why'd you leave him lyin' out there in a downpour like this?"

George considered Constable Porter, whom he had known for twelve or fifteen years. Then he said, "Because, Jud, he's all squashed and strung out, him and his horse, and we didn't have anything to fetch them back in—like a wagon." George held out the reins to his horse and the lawman unconsciously accepted them. George then nodded briskly and turned to walk past, on his way out into the deluged yard on his way to the main-house where he could obtain dry clothing. But that was not his reason for going up there.

Back in the barn Ben Chavez grinned at the dumbfounded look on the lawman's face as he stood there holding George Wayland's horse. Porter saw that and snarled at Ben. "What's so damned funny?"

Ben turned to begin off-saddling as he said, "Nothing, Constable."

The doctor was with Samantha Rockwell and Johnny Welton was hovering in the hallway outside the closed door. When George came along Johnny looked at his disreputable condition then said, "She's doing right well. The doctor said we did just about what should have been done for her."

George nodded, started past in the direction of his own bedroom to get out of the soaked clothing, then turned back and said, "Johnny; Cliff and Jim have any trouble?"

"Not a speck of it," answered the cowboy.

"Then suppose you go over to the cookshack and see

if you can rassel up something to eat for Ben and me."

Welton nodded and unhappily departed, having to finally relinquish his role as guardian of the sick-room door, a function he, nor anyone else for that matter, had to perform.

George smiled crookedly as Johnny turned away. The sick-room door opened, the grizzled medical practitioner from Cibola looked out, stared at George, at his soggy, filthy condition, then sighed and said, "If you want the pneumonia, Mister Wayland, just stay in those clothes, otherwise after you've dried out and redressed Miss Rockwell would like a word with you."

George shouldered past the doctor into the sick-room.

Samantha looked more handsome than she had ever seemed before. Her hair had been brushed until it shone, then twisted ingeniously around her head, and her face was bright with good color. She did not look like someone who had been shot through.

She gave George the same blank stare the doctor had given him, and which he now ignored as he pulled over a chair and sat soggily down, smiling at the handsome girl.

She finally said, "I'll wait, if you'd prefer getting into something dry, Mister Wayland."

He ignored that offer to say, "You look much better. In fact you look so much better if I didn't know differently I'd say you were never shot. . . . The man who shot you died under a stampede. I'm sorry . . . Well; I'm sorry if you are, but otherwise I'll never miss Buster Munser."

She digested this slowly. Whatever her actual feelings

towards the dead man, and whatever their relationship had been, she was more sensitive than Ben Chavez, and *he* had thought Munser had died a terrible death.

"Otherwise," he informed her, "we brought most of your cattle back towards the home-place—and it's raining out. Miss Samantha, by gawd it's raining out!"

She watched his face as she also listened to his voice, and when next she spoke she said, "You sound very pleased. I don't blame you, I'm pleased too . . . My father will pay for the grass and we'll move off the herd the first moment we can—in the morning even if it's still storming. And about those things I said to you in the cookshack—I'm sorry. I really didn't mean them anyway, but I'm sorry I said them."

He stood up leaving a dark puddle where he had been sitting. "There is something you could do for me, Samantha."

"All right. What is it?"

"Just stay exactly as you are until I've cleaned up and fetched a couple of plates from the cookshack, then have supper with me right here."

She smiled. "I'm hungry as a cub bear, Mister Wayland."

He nodded. As for that "mister" business, maybe the opportunity would arise while they were eating to bring that up. Maybe she might agree with him that it sounded as though he were a very old man, when she called him "Mister Wayland."

He went to the door, winked, saw her wink back, and stepped outside where the doctor was coolly lighting a small black cigar as he eyed George and said, "She has the constitution of a buffalo, the strength of a horse, and the disposition of my late wife—who never shirked a day of living in the time allotted to her. On top of that, Mister Wayland, she worries. All afternoon she was sending that cowboy named Welton out to see if there was any sign of you, yet."

George smiled. "I worry a little too, Doctor. Is she in any danger?"

The older man shook his head. "Not from the wound, Mister Wayland, but I can't say what her chances are of surviving whatever it is I can smell cooking in the cookshack."

They grinned at each other and George went along to his bedroom and sat down to change. He just sat, for a moment, feeling tired all the way through for the first time in days. Tired and elated and just a little bit hopeful; it was beginning to appear that the impossible was upon the verge of becoming possible, not in just one case, that of the end of a two-year drought, but in several other incidents also.

He smiled to himself and slowly began to organize his thoughts, and to also change his clothes.

Center Point Publishing
600 Brooks Road ● PO Box 1
Thorndike ME 04986-0001 USA

(207) 568-3717

US & Canada:
1 800 929-9108